The Loss of the
Miraculous

Prose Series 32

Ben Morreale

THE LOSS
OF THE
MIRACULOUS

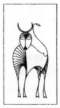

G u e r n i c a
Toronto / New York / Lancaster
1997

Printed in Canada
Typeset by Calista, Toronto.

Antonio D'Alfonso, Editor
Guernica Editions Inc.
P.O. Box 117, Station P, Toronto (ON), Canada M5S 2S6
250 Sonwil Drive, Buffalo, New York 14225-5516 U.S.A.
Gazelle, Falcon House, Queen Square, Lancaster LA1 1RN U.K.

Legal Deposit — First Quarter
National Library of Canada
Library of Congress Catalog Card Number: 95-82276

Canadian Cataloguing in Publication Data
Morreale, Ben
The loss of the miraculous : a novel
(Prose series ; 32)
1 st ed.
ISBN 1-55071-019-2
I. Title   II. Series.
PS3563.O8728L68 1995 813'.54 C95-920849-6
97 98 99 10 9 8 7 6 5 4 3 2 1

For my Beloved Wife
Linda Rogers Morreale
(1939-1995)

Prologue

Put this bottle of chamgagne in the refrigerator and later I'll tell you how and why I won it.

No, thanks, I can't drink armagnac anymore; I know Gurdjieff used to like it, but he's dead now and we're alive. After a while your liver just can't take those cooked wines anymore. I've done my share of drinking armagnac. No use being hoggish. But you go ahead, your young stomach can take it.

I must tell you, though, I always suspected that Gurdjieff was a charlatan. I don't mean that in a bad way, but any prophet who drank armagnac must have been a bit of a charlatan, in spite of the fact that he was looking for the miraculous and found it in the most common places. Well, you think he did. I wish I could feel the way you do about him. One thing happens to you as you grow old, or older, anyway; time becomes a gentleman and things look the same to you coming and going. But then in my Mediterranean town all the prophets are dead, and if one by chance had survived he'd be ignored.

I used to drive from the Valley of the Temples to Port Empedocles then on to my Mediterranean town where a master painter lived, every day for six months, and I knew I was bored with that loveliest of drives when the road looked the same coming and going. And I envy you if you can believe Gurdjieff — that you can wake up beside your wife each morning as if it were the first day — that is miraculous. I know one thing, it takes the consent of two generations to change things.

I don't disagree with you — it's worse. I can't agree with you. I can't consent to what you believe about Gurdjieff. You have found a master and I only find friends. Some find the miraculous, others lose it — and so forth and so on . . .

No, give the champagne some more time. It's a good bottle. My friend William, who had never heard of Gurdjieff, went to much trouble to find it. A good bottle, in spite of its name, Napoleon Champagne. It comes from a small house around Epernay — not far from Bar-le-duc. I knew the marquise who ran the firm — she was a wise woman. She produced only about 400 bottles. I know because I used to play cards with her while we drank a clear green wine from the bottles that had lost their effervescence because the corks had not been set just right. It was a good wine; it reddened your ears. My friend William had to go to the city to find a bottle, and it cost him $18.95.

I never heard you talk about Gurdjieff and what he had to say of growing old. My friend lost his bottle of champagne because, as he said, he could not live without some lyricism in his life — and that's just another way of saying he had to have the miraculous in his life. But even the miraculous, after a while, gets to look the same coming and going. I made a bet with him and he lost. I just wanted to make it a bottle of red wine. But he became more and more certain he would win and he kept raising the bet. A bottle of chablis, he said; I said, O.K. Then the champagne. How did I know he was going to lose? Well, I was hoping he'd win. I wasn't about to drink to his sorrow. I told him that.

We began to have dinner together, the three of us — William, Brian Davis, and myself — about four years ago, every Wednesday night at a restaurant by the lake. One of those places that smells winter damp up to the last day of November when it closed. In the winter we ate at Raoul's in town. We had dinner with wine in about an hour and a half and then left, after talking about politics, sports — usually baseball — but most of all we talked about women. Not in a vulgar way, because my friend liked lyricism. But just about relationships. Without knowing it, we were trying to understand why men fall in love. Brian Davis needed women and yet feared them. My friend, though, truly loved women, which is rare for big men who usually are indifferent or cruel to them. My friend William always made me marvel, you know. And I'd ask him, "What is this thing that men have about women?"

The wine made me sentimental.

William had been married twice. I don't know why they had not worked out. He never told me and I never asked. Although I think it had to do with the loss of lyricism.

When we started having dinners together, my friend was living with a very nice woman named Nancy. They were good friends. My friend loved her two children. His house was often filled with people who just stopped by. Nancy was busy with teaching, and my friend with work he liked very much. In the evenings he painted and was becoming quite good at it. That is, he could stand before a canvas for hours and learn great truths about a rose, Nancy's naked- ness, and his own face. He did that painting over there of warm rocks in the sun. Brian calls them hot rocks.

We had only one rule about our dinners: we would not invite any women. Although the year Brian Davis was away in India we broke that rule. One evening in April my friend came to dinner look- ing distraught. Usually he was pretty easy going, not that he was always that way. He simply had learned to be calm, although in the time I knew him I had never seen him angry. I shouldn't say that — he did get angry with men in high places and called one of them tricky wart face.

We had talked about Jeanne — Jean pro- nounced in the French manner, really — the week before. Brian had introduced them. She was twenty- three. But I don't think it was that she was young, and he old. My friend had gone through that; at forty- two he had married a twenty-two-year old girl, and six months later she had left him with a Newfound- land pup named Adam. My friend wasn't upset.

With Jeanne it was something else. He said that she was the most intelligent girl he had ever met and that she would get better. He never tired of talking to her and he never tired of looking at her.

It had not begun that way. Jeanne had been having difficulty "sexually," as she said. Her experiences
had left her weeping. "I felt like the urinals in the
John in some bus station."

Her friends had suggested Brian, who was good
in such matters, but he was busy beyond any human
capacity just then. It was Brian who introduced
Jeanne to my friend, so he said.

The next Wednesday my friend explained the
situation to me in disbelief, really. "The dew appeared on her upper lip four, five times . . . she
stirred my honey five, six times." He was very lyrical.

He told me of his instructing her, and we talked
of the poignancy of mixing generations — that in
such love, teaching became so intensified until no
one knew who taught and who learned.

For a few Wednesdays he did not talk of Jeanne.
Then, on a Tuesday he called and asked if I would
mind if he brought her to our dinner.

She was lovely. She had auburn hair which was
sometimes red and other times amber. She was radiant. Her face was tight and shining, water-washed, as
they said in my Mediterraen town. Her eyes were a
grey-green with splinters of strange colors.

That Wednesday they just sat there holding
hands and looking at each other. I kidded them as we
left, and Jeanne said, "Oh, I'm sorry, I'm sorry," with
happy embarrassment.

For the next three weeks William did not speak
of Jeanne. His beard became richer and redder, his

hair fuller. He began to wear cuff links. He had discovered the miraculous.

Now Gurdjieff says there are four bodies, doesn't he? The Carnal, the Natural, the Spiritual and the Divine. There was no doubt — my friend was in the Divine.

The marquise, who was forty-two when we drank the clear green wine, told me that women at twenty-three have a great sense of survival.

That summer William had to be away, and I returned to visit my Mediterranean town as I often do. When we resumed our Wednesday dinners in the fall my friend William did not speak of Jeanne until a month had passed and then he simply said, "She has gone back to one of her jocks." And he would not say another word about it. Around Thanksgiving he said, "Jeanne is leaving."

"I'm sorry to hear that," I told my friend.

"She'll be leaving around Christmas, but she'll come to see me before she goes."

"No, she won't," I said.

"Yes, she will. She will," he said.

"What do you want to bet?" I said.

Nothing really terrible happened to my friend. His beard in a matter of weeks grew dull and grey as if he had stopped dyeing it. His hair thinned out and lay flat on his head. His eyes grew dull. His teeth that were white and square remained so, almost as a reminder of the lyricism he had lost.

Now, let's open the bottle of champagne and drink to him, for I promised him I wouldn't drink to his sorrow, but share it with people I liked.

1

Such a thing could not have happened between my friend William and Jeanne in my Mediterranean town — time has exhausted the land, men withdraw to families for comfort. Such emotions are too costly.

Brian had not introduced Jeanne to my friend. "You've got the wrong idea," he said almost angrily. "Brian had nothing to do with it."

My friend was going to the city one afternoon on business and since he disliked driving he took the bus. He first saw Jeanne, he told me, when she came into the waiting room followed by Bob carrying her bag. What had struck him at the time was the mournful way Bob had kissed Jeanne. "Like a hang-dog man, married for twenty years, instead of one who had lived with her only six months."

It was his curiosity about Bob's gesture that made him talk to her. They quickly became engrossed in talk about books, all those books the young love. My friend discovered that she was not just an empty-headed pretty face and that love does come as a surprise.

He listened to her stories of her travels and to his surprise he also felt a compassion. He told her stories of his life and she found comfort. They were hardly aware that the bus had broken down, nor that another bus had come one hour later. The world around them seemed to fade and shrink until only the two of them remained, wrapped in a cocoon, spun of their eyes, knowingly — the pull of discovery and their sudden desire to touch one another — a lyrical blur.

"I'm glad I met you," my friend said as he left, and she took his arm and hugged it. "So am I."

"The parting was a bursting of the cocoon that transformed us both," he told me.

2

Can there be lyricism in a town where there are no donkeys, mules or horses — in a town where there are no animals but pets?

In this town there is a Bohemian quarter with an empty lot on the corner and a wall painted with a country scene — a house, a road, and an American flag in the foreground. On top, Ma Cokelie advertises a breakfast for $1.98 as "America's finest cooking."

A midget stands in front of Ma Cokelie's, leaning on a crooked cane, his eyes blood-shot, watching broken heartedly while a long legged girl goes by — his hands in his pocketless pants where a fragile bird flutters.

In my Mediterranean town the birds fly free among the medlar trees. In the winter, young boys trap them and roast them over twigs of thyme and eat them while they talk vulgarly about women.

3

I've forgotten the name of the first man I met in this town. Yet I remember his nicotine-gold fingers with square turned up nails. "We're on loan to each other," he used to say, and walk around this town in an aimless way. He saw no one, and yet he hunched his shoulders as if everyone were looking at him. He fell in love with a young girl and the impossibility of the love, in that time, gnawed at him so much that on his birthday he sent letters to his eighteen-year-old son, his sixteen-year-old daughter and to his wife Lucinda. Then he drove to a quiet place by Lake Vernon, hooked a hose from the exhaust to an opening in the front window, started the engine, and from behind the steering wheel watched the evening light fade.

To his eighteen-year-old son he wrote, "Excuse me please, excuse this. I'm at a dead end and yet I see the fields beyond." To his daughter he wrote tenderly. To his wife he wrote, "Lucinda, you know I have nothing to write, nothing. You just can't pay the mortgage anymore."

4

This town was once lovely. Just above the railroad station where Jeanne lived for a while, the ground was covered with larkspur, poppies, spieria and babies' breath, and in late summer when time grew lazy queen anne's lace with black lentils in their centers grew up an embankment to the high-ceilinged mansions. It was a young town and men cared for it as if they knew it would outlast the lake itself.

Now, you see, those flowered embankments are gone and the high-ceilinged mansions have been divided into five and six apartments. The railroad station is closed. The trucks rumble through the once quiet street on their way to the oil depot. This town was once better than it is now. In each car there is only one man, and the sidewalks are disappearing.

5

In that time, when the bombers roared in fields beside the lake to fly off for weekend bommbings in the distant war, the girls were fucking themselves to death and it broke the hearts of the older people. It was not, as the younger said, that "the grey beards are just jealous."

No, it just broke their hearts.

Jeanne had told me of that night in May when voices shouted, "They're killing students." She stood stoned, watching a Domino's Pizza truck run by, wondering if it would turn up seven or craps next time. Her man grew pale from the pills he had taken, and shivered because he thought the eagle on top of the town monument was becoming a sword directed at his heart. She comforted him until she felt compelled to take to the streets herself and walk with thousands of others, holding a candle, beside a friend who kept muttering, "I've got to do more; this is not enough. Stop the fucking war," and then suddenly began to sob. "Where is Vietnam! I can't go on with this shit! I can't go on." She tried to get him to move, but he just sat down and waited. When she waited with him, they were both arrested.

Jeanne had sung in all the funerals in her home town and had seen death as a ceremony. That summer she strapped an orange colored pack to her back and went to Europe. "I had to get away. I was confused." To bring pleasure to the men in Europe.

Her stories broke my heart.

6

I'm not used to the sound of these four lettered words and can't bring myself to use them openly. In my Mediterranean town they have always been used with the frankness of the women who scoop out their milk swollen breasts to feed an infant who soon falls asleep, his hand warding off the heaviness. I can use those lively words in the language of my Mediterra-

17

nean town, as freely as a poor old woman who no longer has jewels or her virginity to lose. But I was brought up in this town, and to use these words in this language makes me sometimes blush.

7

In my Mediterranean town the men danced in halls run by a virtuous man. There were no women. The owner sold tickets from a large wheel and when enough men were let into the hall he would play a tango, a waltz or a fox trot. The men, some awkwardly, others elegantly, danced in the dimly lit hall with its cement floor to the hollow sound of a hand-wound phonograph.

They were men in their thirties and forties — "old capons," the aging priest called them, who in lust had never seen the breast of a woman, let alone the navel.

Whenever a man returned to town from a distant city, the conversation in the dance hall arrived at things that mattered.

"Is it true that one can dance with women where you've been?"

"Yes."

"In the afternoon?"

"Yes, even in the afternoon."

Silence.

"Can you walk with a woman in the streets alone, without her mother or an aunt?"

"Yes."

Silence. They all averted their eyes.

Then a man of forty or so asked, "Tell me, what does a woman's breast feel like?"

The music started up again. The men glided along in each other's arms. Their eyes half closed, their lips stretched tight, all danced a little more elegantly, the thoughts of women too much with them.

8

Brian said that he had slept with 170 women and, because as he said, he was into photography, he had photographed many of them. "Every woman wants to be photographed," he said. He had thick sheafs of photographs of women he had made love to. He kept them in large folders left over from his work.

He would set up his camera beside the bed, set the timer and quickly jump to a pose. No doubt because he was interested in history he had set them in a chronological order. And in those pictures I could see him growing to maturity, putting on weight, and the pictures changing from the surprised faces who had to pose for time exposures to the customary sex manual photographs, to close-ups that at first were biological, and then in the latest folders ticketed, for some reason "Sacco and Vanzetti," were all close-ups of cunts. There were pink cunts, liver brown ones, mussel pink, eggplant purple ones, sea urchin rose ones. One was ash-grey and each one more closely photographed than the other. The last pictures were such close-ups that one would not know what they were if not told; one could imagine them to be pictures of lava from some volcano in my Mediterranean town with its scarlet folds slowly turning over and its center dark and smoking. The last photograph was simple darkness. He had brought the camera so close that nothing could be seen. I don't know what he was looking for in that darkness.

I know I often saw those men in my Mediterranean town who had never seen a woman's navel but in the darkness of their imaginations.

9

A young man once left my Mediterranean town to become a famous writer in the cities of the world. When he was forty eight he returned to spend the mornings at his desk and the afternoons walking in the town square with the men of leisure and power, and of course the old. From time to time men of letters came from the cities to ask about his work. The writer walked with them in the square and talked to them of almond trees and the price of wheat. When he died at eighty, these men went to his writing table and found a large pile of papers. On the top page was written, "The gap between a work of art and my ability is too great." The rest were blank.

This story haunted a master-painter who had returned to my Mediterranean town after having become world renowned. He was a slight man with full lips and the face of a young pony whose drinking had given him a ruddy complexion which, from a distance, seemed like the suntan of a rich man. He had made the tour of cities not far from this town and in one, where he exhibited his paintings, a man had come in, glanced at them and bought every one. The painter had made a great deal of money in that city and had learned to drink whiskey by the tumbler.

Now he lived in an abandoned theater where each morning he hammered canvas to his frames and in the afternoon he walked in the square, arm in arm, with the men of my Mediterranean town, listening to their stories and telling them of his adventures all over the world.

10

Jeanne used to call my friend William each morning around Ten. By nine-thirty he was already agitated. He would turn on his radio and pace the length of the room, clapping his hands gently to the repetitious rhythm. By nine-forty-five he was snapping his fingers and doing graceful pirouettes over his Persian carpet. By nine-fifty he began to trim his beard neatly. By ten he was pacing in long swinging steps.

When by five past ten, if the phone had not rung, he was almost frightened. At ten-ten he felt his heart beating in his temples. He tried dancing, but stumbled. His heart was not in it. It was in his throat and in his temples. At ten-fifteen, a sadness made his body vibrate. The phone rang and he was in the midst of joy which to him was an exhilaration without excitement.

Jeanne would meet him on the far side of the bridge that crossed the River Dunbar. She would look up at him only when she was half way across. Each morning she came with a poem she had written the night before.

Long after that, when Jeanne was away, between nine-thirty and ten-thirty my friend was filled with a loneliness that was like the wind. But still his head bobbed up and down happily to a tune, as if in the silence he remembered.

We spanned three different times — Brian, my friend William and me. I was the oldest, Brian the youngest, and my friend the bridge.

11

Debrah was so much in love with Brian that she saw a blue aura about him, and everything this aura touched she loved the tables and chairs in his house by the lake, his car and his friends. Since, at that time, Brian and my friend shared the house by the lake, it was very easy for Debrah to go out on Sunday afternoons and loll about the house, naked beneath Brian's multicolored silk kimona and read the *Sunday Times* with William, about the floor, the couch and sometimes in the upstairs room. While outside the winter wind ran veinlike over the snow drifts covering the hard frozen lake and through the pine trees set out to mark a safe passage to the Dunbar River.

Debrah comforted William that winter and in the spring she said to me, "A man like Brian should not make love to a girl when she is only nineteen. It's not fair, not fair at all."

12

From the high road the ground fell off suddenly in swollen terraces of grass and violet wild phlox, to commemorate some ancient life that lay buried there and where in early summer men came with flashlights late at night looking for night crawlers. I often sit on the lowest swell, by the telephone pole just above the round cut stone, the remnants of a fountain, and watch the bridge.

It's an old iron bridge, heavy and complexly spun in a time when men loved iron, they had been the first to see its possibilities and none of its flaws. Certainly it was love and affection that spanned the Dunbar River with so much iron so that at best two people could walk across its plank-covered trestles. Now, the bend of the river is almost hidden by flowering locust trees and tall dying elms that half-hide the bright new sign: *Keep out — pedestrians bicycles and fishermen*. To the left of the bridge are six dark poplars all in a row, their roots deep in the river.

In early summer I sit by the round stone and watch the bridge across the Dunbar River smooth and stretched tight as a slate-colored drum. A long puff of wind makes the poplar leaves tremble with a brittle sharpness — mandolin picks — and the surface of the river is suddenly alive with reflected light and dark chatter. Only beneath the bridge is the water still and deep.

By the old round stone the flashlights gleam. The men are looking for worms. They pass. In the center of the stone where once the fountain's water flowed I find an almost full pack of cigarettes and a snake ring of old gold. Who has crossed that brooding bridge to leave me abandoned vices? It's terrible to be in love and have a premonition that you are dying, but then the fear of dying and the fear of loving are neighbors in the village of the mind.

13

The seats had all been taken out of the theater where the painter lived. In the early days of his return, he would sit in the empty theater listening to the recordings of opera and drinking tumblers of whiskey until he began to dance the wild dances he had learned in his travels far from his town. His hand behind his head, his chest puffed out, he started slowly, encouraging himself with whimpers, little cries, shouts, screams and bits of opera arias. He stamped the ground and whirled around the empty stage until he fell exhausted and crying in the darkness of a deserted but once luxurious loge. The widow Grace's son, who brought him fruits and vegetables, often found him cold and sweaty among his empty canvases. The painter had been a hero in a war against a native tyrant and often told stories of that time in the paintings that had made him wealthy and famous. "I've painted the same picture over and over again. I'm tired," he often said when he fell in a heap after his dance. "You learn nothing in a war. Don't let those imbeciles tell you that you get used to it. The only thing you learn is that the longer it lasts, the more frightened you become. It's much like life."

14

"What day is it today?" the painter would ask the widow Grace's son, in spite of the fact that he had calendars in the dressing rooms he used as his quarters.

"The 20th of March," the boy would say sullenly.

"Eeh, but what year, what year?"

The boy would tell him and this would calm him. "There's time then, there's time?"

He repeated this often with many people, as if the ritual were important to him.

15

In my Mediterranean town the carts were once painted with scenes of past conflicts in dark vivid colors that even now stand out against the hot yellow sky. The widow's husband had been a carter, driving his carts loaded with sulphur down to the one-sailed ships rocking in the sea.

The widow's son was apprenticed to an old man who still made the carts, bending the wood over hot steaming barrels into wheels, the boy beside him, serious, handing him tools with supple, twig-like fingers.

When the boy came with his provisions and found the painter surrounded by tightly stretched and empty canvases, he asked, as a thirteen-year old boy would, "When are you going to paint on them?"

"When the tribunal in my head tells me how I can hide myself in a painting," he said.

16

The first year the master-painter returned to my Mediterranean town, the idle men — and there were many — came to see him each afternoon, casually, as if they had simply interrupted their strolling in the square. To their greeting of "What do you say, master," he would invariably answer, "I can't complain," then add, "it does no good."

This soon became a signal that they could stay and he would tell them stories of his travels, of the many women he had known, and of his fighting during the war. He ended with, "You learn nothing in a war, nothing. The only thing you learn is that the longer it lasts, the more frightened you become. It's much like life."

Rituals are a comfort in my Mediterranean town.

17

I was surprised that love could come to Brian Davis. It seemed to me that the time to which he was born had lost the sense of mindless love that I and my friend William were prone to, that his time believed it important to remain calm, to play it cool, as they said.

Brian had this idea that he could hide from love in its very midst. I think that's why he lit from woman to woman like a firefly in a crystal hive, each one a reflection of the other, a piece of each here and there reflected, in the other. He felt safe this way. Love would never find him if he hid within its very folds. He became a gymnast of fornication until his organs swelled like cobble stones and he felt safe in his unsuspecting laughter. He was tall and lithe and yet with a hint of lustful heaviness that some men have in their early thirties. His boyish face was covered with a thick brown and gold beard. "Honey Lips," Debrah once had called him.

There was no rhyme or reason to it when he met Chris. Within a week — no, two — he began to look like a Neapolitan tenor about to burst into tearful song. If you touched his arm, he jumped and a flower picked could make him talk about the meaning of life. The shimmering lake made him silent. He became gentle, spoke of Chris's intelligence, showed us her baby pictures, and from time to time muttered, "Life is a fucking thing, isn't it?" He left for India soon after to seek the essence and perfection.

The fireflies could have told him more.

18

Chris had a small soft mouth whose lips, just before she began speaking, opened up like a flower to expose a curled tongue each time she said such words as *look*, *lick* or *luck*.

Chris found Brian among his women, routed him out. She slept with men as easily as he slept with women, making sure to tell him — casually. She once had been a nun and had left the convent to marry an older man who had died soon after they both came to our town. Now at age thirty-four she had the air of a suffering widow so appealing to Brian. It made him feel as if he cuckold the very dead and reaffirmed his own life. But you take everything of a woman to bed with you. And with Chris, Brian took her inherited wealth and her gracious home, with soft lighting and a toilet broad and low that flushed so quietly that one was hypnotized by the swirling silent waters. He took her frenzy to bed with him.

She outplayed him with the madness that lay beneath her sweet smile, and encouraged his panic when he realized that she was equal to him, that she was outplaying him. His panic often burst out in rage and anger against my friend William or me.

It didn't happen often, usually when Chris called him from someone else's bed. A day or two later after Chris told him, casually, all the details of her fucking, he would be gentle and kind to Chris and to all of us, hardly aware of her voluptuous use of jealousy to tie him to her.

In my Mediterranean town they would have said she was possessed of the Demons — *incubus* and *sucubus* — that her evil was not banal. It was an obsession. Her ability to make love to both men and women was proof of that. Her own inability to feel jealousy at anything Brian did would seen unnatural.

In my Mediterranean town they would have noticed her small sharp teeth, her body that seemed to have no bones — only a back bone.

She left her teeth marks on the shoulders of everyone she made love to. Two such women could kill any man or woman. A school of such demons would leave only the bare bones.

19

Around the bridge, timing for a lovely light is so important. The sun must be at the right angle, the trees almost leafless, the temperature around 68° F.; then, the sheen on the Dunbar River as it flows down to the Lake Vernon is unbearably hopeful. The bridge for a moment throbs with dappled light and the sheen is gone — voices fade into the night . . .

"Put your head above my heart."

"I hate the beating of a heart."

"Why?"

"It reminds me of death."

"My but you are romantic," the woman's voice says. To be aware of that lovely light diminishing is a sad comfort; to be told is no comfort at all. You can't fabricate the sheen on which you think you could skim your memory like a flat green stone and arrive at a place as safe as home.

20

Love must be a demon's gift — given in a moment of remorse but still a demon's gift. It cannot be a gift from God. It is a torment consumated in pain with breathless cries of anguish and sorrow, and moans of past hungers of the soul. God Himself would weep if He could find deep within Him the cosmic seed that made the demon.

In the vicinity of my Mediterranean town Jeanne, her orange pack on her back, met a man who once had danced in my town's womanless halls. "He was kind and attentive," Jeanne told me, "even jealous, of the stupid things I did. I felt more female then, than ever. We spent a fabulous night together. He left early in the morning. In the afternoon I saw him in the square and he would not even talk to me. That night he came with friends and they all took turns fucking me. I didn't care. I didn't care at all. I just didn't understand how he had changed."

"He had thought of women all his life, Jeanne," I told her. "How could anyone, any woman, come up to twenty years of imagining. Even you. It's all in the head, you know. He must have hated you for a moment."

Jeanne looked at me, just then, like an attentive fox.

21

The painter quickly became known for his stories, and in a town where so many could not read or found reading so difficult as to make it a bore, this was no small thing. His stories attracted some almost as a challenge — above all, the old story teller of the town, an old man, blind now, who had once gone from village to village telling stories of pirates who had come from the sea.

The story the men liked most of all was the story of The Girl, the God and Death. The painter said that it had happened to him. They never tired of hearing it. So much so that the painter would tell it on the Feast-Day of the Dead and then over a period of three days. This ritual became part of the story.

22

In our town two old ladies lived in one of the grand old mansions just above the railroad station. They were both in their nineties and why the word *love* upset them so I never did understand.

Elvira, the elder (she was ninty-three), had studied the piano with Litischinsky, who just could not understand the modernity of Debussy. She lived with Alice Mary Humble, who had once read her poetry to pink-faced insurance brokers in Chicago to the rhythm of a new music called Jazz. Together they ran a music school. Elvira's motto was: *You want to play the piano seriously, don't get married*. "Marriage is a snare. It just wasn't meant for piano players. The only marriage I've known to work is a marriage without sex," she said, nodding her head rhythmically.

Elvira had lived with Alice Mary's husband before the first great war and the three of them had lived contentedly until his death soon after the second great war.

"The world will be put right," she often repeated to me when I visited them on the porch of their old house, "when all are female, when the need for men, the male, will be done away with."

"But who will write of Romeo and Juliet?" I asked. "And what will become of Dante and Beatrice, Abelard and Eloise? And how will we live with one another in the meantime?"

"I'm not a creative person," Elvira said, "I'm only a teacher of piano, and if you want to play the piano seriously, don't marry. And if you do, get rid of the sex thing."

Alice Mary, ninty-one, with a halo of gnats round her head, sat in the converted chapel where they lived nodding to the tempo of Elvira's words. Around the wall were pictures of women playing tennis in long white bloomers. On the floor beside Elvira were two tennis rackets.

In Alice Mary's glasses, thick as magnifying lenses, I could see reflections of the bridge. I was reminded I had come to ask them to be character witnesses for Jeanne's husband Bob, who had been arrested and faced the possibility of ten years in prison — shortly after he, and Jeanne had married.

23

In that time it seemed to me I had done everything — everything Brian was to do and everything my friend had done.

It wasn't restlessness I felt, it was worse somehow, and rather than go to bed I went to see Brian who had just spent his first winter in his house by the Lake Vernon.

There had been heavy snows that winter, thaws and snows again, so that to cut through a foot of snow was to see the history of that winter's weather.

The juniper bushes around Brian's house were buried in snow. But in the past four days an unusual thaw had set in and then, just as suddenly, the weather had turned fiercely cold again.

This early April night was starlit as I walked the deeply rutted back road to Brian's house. In the upstairs room I could see the red light, muffled by acrylic curtains and the tall bearded shadow of Brian clinging to a shorter shadow — a butterfly in pain whose motions had no middle, only starts and ends.

The window opened and I heard their laughter as something came sailing out of the window and landed among the juniper bushes, fluttered there for a while and then fell limp to the ground. Behind me the headlights of a car appeared nodding slowly on the washboard road, illuminating the winter's debris the recent thaw had turned up. For a moment, there in the car's headlights I thought I saw dead worms; some had caught in the bushes and their bodies filled with thawed and frozen snow now looked like sacks of exotic fruit with frozen wax-like tips; others were delicate, crushed coil springs or old teabags.

The car came closer. As I moved back to let it pass, my foot stepped into the debris and a frozen lump softly burst beneath my weight. I looked down and saw that I had crushed a used condom. The ground around me was covered with them. Some were on the wreck of an abandoned car; one, worm-like, peered half out of the frozen ground.

The car was almost on me now. The waxen seed beneath my foot just then turned red, as the car's tail lights went by and trailed off into the night.

The stars were like confetti that clear cold night and before I took my first step home I wondered how long it took a dead star's light to fade before our eyes. I took a careful step out of Brian's yard and started home. The step was careful, because I suddenly thought — "In my Mediterranean town, would any-one believe, if they were told, in the existence of such landscapes."

24

"Sometimes I look at the sky on winter nights and I think the universe is a prolonged orgasm," Brian told me one Wednesday evening. He went on to ex-plain. "You know that men who can see such things say the planets and the stars are moving away from us. The universe is a process — a universe in the process of exploding. And when the outer limit of the explosion is reached gravity will pull the universe to-gether again. Bang out — ten billion years. Gravity in — ten million years. They call it the accordion theory. I prefer to think the godesses are fucking — godlessly — a cosmic fuck. Sometimes I look at the sky on win-ter nights and I think the universe is just a prolonged orgasm of the female gods and a man's head is in his cock."

25

Why the painter had come back to my Mediterranean town no one knew. The priest said he lacked tranquility of spirit. Some said it was because of a woman, still others, because of politics.

"Why does he drink so much?"

"And why does he live alone in the theater? I would go crazy in a place like that. All alone, with all the spirits of such a place."

No one saw the painter work, although it was rumored that the dressing rooms were filled with hundreds of magnificent paintings.

"How do you know that?" one man would ask.

"Eeh, because of the strong odor of paint I always smell."

"That's the whiskey."

"Whiskey does not smell like that."

"How do you know it doesn't?"

"I have traveled."

And the men continued to pace in the square down to the Mother Church, and back to the café at the other end.

26

The widow still had a fine water-washed complexion, as they say, a strong and mournful face which for some reason gave her the nickname of the Lady Pharoh.

Soon after her husband's death she became the town whore, not only because of a widow's poverty but out of arrogance. She told no one of her suffering in seeing her son grow up sullen in a town that valued virginity and fidelity even beyond the grave. Yet, it would have finished badly for the Lady Pharoh and her son, if she hadn't come under the protection of a young priest. Afterwards, she practiced the art of midwifery, walking the streets alone day or night with her bag of herbs, jars of leeches, oils, wicks, glass cups and old copper coins for those who suffered.

If any asked, "But aren't you afraid to walk the streets alone?" she would answer, "Eeh, afraid of what? I have neither jewels nor virginity to lose, you know."

The widow often brought provisions for the painter. He would dance and sing for her until he fell in a heap, crying among his empty canvases. She helped him up and took him to the back rooms.

"*The mad dancers have set up house keeping in my head again,*" the lady Irish poet said to me once. How or why she came or ended up in our town no one knew, not even my friend William who once out of delicacy attempted to make love to this thirty-seven year old virgin. William who was kindly in such matters gently ran his hands up her blouse to fondle her dixie cup breasts only to have her grow cold, half faint. She put her head between her legs, bobbing, until revived, she rushed to the window and wept.

Often when my friend William walked his New-foundland dog along the river's edge down to the bridge I'd meet him and he would recognize me only when I was face to face with him. I knew that Jeanne was still too much with him. He'd walk about the bridge, stand by it, touch its railing and talk about this town made of the spare parts from every corner of the world.

He put his foot upon the bridge and looked across the river. "They've set up housekeeping in my head again — the mad dancers."

The lady Irish poet was our third character witness.

28

So you've both come with more armagnac and talk of Gurdjieff, and I can only talk of my friend and Jeanne.

Yes, he saw Jeanne again, but only much later, almost a year after we had drunk to his loss of the miraculous. She hadn't gone off with a jock but with a cocky pink-faced boy whose silky hair she loved to touch. Jeanne had spent the summer in the woods and, then, with her mother, alone and brooding. When Bob, that pink-faced boy, came and told her he needed her, she said, "Fuck it. I'm tired," and they were married. Only her mother knew of their marriage. They returned to this town to live in those apartments close to Elvira and Alice Mary in such isolation that no one knew they were there.

In that time my friend had grown acrid, there was the smell of sour dough about him. Once he had told me that while taking a shower he had caught a whif of Jeanne's smell "of vanilla and the loins of some wild animal," he said. "I hate to take showers now."

I often saw him walking grimly, in that time before he saw Jeanne again, pulled by his last wife's dog. Only when he saw me would his face light up as he shouted my name.

"Friend," I'd answer, "How are you?"

He'd look grim again and talk to me of poetry — of Arnold and Tennyson — inappropriate men to read once a man believes he has blown his chances out of hand. But he insisted and quoted Arnold:

> *Lightly flows our war of words and yet*
> *Behold with tears mine eyes are wet.*

Jeanne had once read them to him. It was no use my telling him that:

> *Men have died from time to time*
> *and worms have eaten them, but not for love,*
> *not for love.*

Not all poets are mad. He felt used, taken advantage of. He was in no mood for Shakespeare. I heard him mutter, "That pig of a woman. They used me — didn't they? — to pump life into a dead relationship. The pig." Strong language for my friend.

At our Wednesday night dinners I tried to comfort him. "It's just approaching forty-nine, the nines are bad. Forty-nine worst of all," I said, and recited Dante's wail:

> *In the middle of my life I found myself*
> *alone and lost beneath a woods so deep*
> *it broke my heart.*

Literature was no remedy. The disease was still with him, and I knew that if she made the slightest sign he would be burning with laughter and joy, bouyed by the miraculous.

When did I grow my beard?

I grew it when we started having dinners to-gether on Wednesday night, five years ago now. We thought it would be amusing, three bearded men, one beard almost blond, my friend's near red, and mine almost white.

But you say I have charisma. No, it's simply that I have lived long enough . . . if you live long enough, you will have it too. You will. Anyway, you know what I am, what I have become and you, good lady, I'll bet you are frightened of him, your man, sometimes, be-cause you don't know what he will become. And that's the excitement and the turmoil.

What was Jeanne like? She was many things then, in the making. She was a princess at seventeen when a sullen fullback scored touchdowns in her name and then she made love to him while her mother was away and after he beat her blue, as foot-ball heroes do. She had experienced much and learned little. But then she walked as if she would never look back.

What was she like really?

She was being formed then by having to choose between reality and the endless lunacy of the De-mon's gift. I think she knew that love can only be experienced once, because it is an insanity, a self-de-vouring one. She had some mad poets to guide her.

All my friend William would talk about was the mixture of the Demon's gift and God's desire. He was very much a man of Tennyson. But then Tennyson and Arnold first saw his world of honesty and gentle-ness and heroism and ethical fucking (pardon me), and my friend was the last to see it. The world will not be seen that way again. Both of you won't, in any case. I'll bet you a bottle of champagne you won't.

You can talk of fucking, of cocks and cunts. My friend calls that sailors' talk, men who have no ties to this earth. You both think he didn't understand that such words have a poetry all their own. That's not so. He knew the power and the beauty of those words. I found that out later. But there's the burr that rubs the buttocks of our minds — to find that mixture of the Demon's fucking gift and God's gentle source of love.

God's source is not gentle, you say?

Well, I know William felt that with Jeanne. Because he felt alone and frightened, and yet, as if a new life were about to begin for him. Love is mixed with Death somehow, isn't it? What was Jeanne like?

Later she was to say to my friend, "I've never wanted to make babies and now with you I do. I do!" She was a rascal, an all-American rascal.

What was Jeanne like?

It would wound my friend to hear her speak of being "fucked up" and that her "dude" had better "get his cock together." It lacerated him to hear her say that her husband stuffed her cunt with cotton. "It's a wound to him; all the openings of my body; they're wounds to him."

What was Jeanne like?

She had become slightly coarse, after living with Bob, her husband. She was becoming like her cocky husband, which was only natural. My friend grieved because he wanted to live with her and have her become like him, and he like her. When she said, "My cunt needs filling and he won't even touch me," my friend wept silently, grimly.

I gave them a small blue key that I had made for them, to use my house during the day. They thanked me and left the house neat — always. Yet to this day I still find strange buttons in the crevices of my chairs, a foot print beside the guest room bed where in summer when the air is still, I catch whiffs of vanilla, urine and the sea.

What was Jeanne really like?

Jeanne never cried. I never saw her eyes in tears. Now, give me some of that armagnac because my heart goes out to them, my friend and Jeanne. I don't think it will end well for them. The dogs are restless and the fireflies glow breathlessly. The omens aren' t good, as they say in my Mediterranean town.

29

In my Mediterranean town the patron saint is St. Anthony who was martyred into his old age by visions of pink buttocks that turned into sows whenever he touched them. But there was the Virgin, too, and Christ. Everyone takes turns adoring them: St. Anthony, the Virgin and Christ, the Infant Christ.

The Festival to the Virgin begins around Memorial Day. Her statue is taken from its niche in the Mother Church of the Annunciation and carried in procession all around the town. The Virgin is childless but her belly is swollen, which prompts one man watching from the steps of the wine cellar to whisper to a boy, as he points to her swollen belly, "What do you think it will be, a boy or a girl?"

In our town on the day of the Feast of the Immaculate Conception, a flag is hoisted up and carried by a trinity of men with guns and crushed army hats. It is adored, this flag, like the image of Christ. No one speaks of the Virgin, let alone of the Christ in her womb, not even the priest-mayor of this town who presses the palm of his hand above his heart each time another flag goes by.

30

I know that my friend would be upset, as it upsets me to tell this about the lawyer Sewall who prepared the case against Jeanne's husband. He was a prim and proper man. He wore a dark brown jacket woven in the style of some Prince of Wales; so was the manner in which he laced his tie. His shoes were always shined and on rainy days he carried his London Fog impermeable to Happy Herman's where he watched the go-go girls — their buttocks to his eyes, pretending love making to the wall.

Lawyer Sewall had two houses, two cars, seven children and one wife. Through the local Grand Old Party he had been given the post of prosecuting attorney. He was elected to the board of education and hoped to be sent to the legislature. He wanted to go, he said, "because it is a challenge." Then, too, he was "desirous of serving the public interest."

Every two months he left for the city where he called a number he kept in the crevices of his wallet, then waited in a suite of rooms. He took a shower, put on a terry cloth bathrobe, as advertised in *Playboy Magazine*, lay back upon the bed and began to read *Atlas Shrugged* by Ayn Rand.

When the girl arrived wearing a well-tailored blue and yellow suit, he knew her gentle air, her large blue eyes set deep within her head as if ashamed. He believed her gentleness to be an act, but he didn't mind. It gave him pleasure. Then, too, all life he told himself was an act.

She seemed rested this time.

Ceremoniously he offered her drambuie. They rubbed noses, lips. He laughed. She whispered, "What would excite you now?"

"I'd like to read a bit."

"From your law books again?"

"I've found a new passage in . . ."

"If you like, then . . ."

While he lay back on the bed propped upon two pillows she undressed, came to him naked, ran her fingers up his legs and then across his stomach. She rolled a rubber device gently on to him, then turned her back to his eyes, and in a gesture as if she were mounting a horse, showed him in a flash her gaping sex, a dark split fig, and mounted him. He saw himself disappear into her darkness.

As he read, the lawyer Sewall could see just above the book her strong round buttocks spread almost flat before him like the podium on which to set Ayn Rand's *Atlas Shrugged*. He began to read:

"What happened?" gasped Chalmers.

"Split rail," the conductor answered impassively.

"The engine went off the track."

"Off?"

"On its side."

The hips before the lawyer Sewall began to move slowly like a piston scooping water from a deep stream, silently — in a professional gesture that understood the tension of pleasure was a slow expectation — and then began his long terrible painful cry. When his cry subsided he gave the buttocks before him, such a blow with his open hand that the girl went sprawling off the bed and on to the floor.

I heard this story from Angelica, a friend of Brian's who danced in the circuit from the city to our town along the Dunbar River.

I wonder where all the love the lawyer Sewall must have had in summer time for his gentle, seven-child bearing wife, where had it all gone, where had he buried it, cremated it? Who had been the undertaker? who had cried for it? who had bought a flat green stone for it? who had carved the book-end dates: born then, died now?; who had buried it? So that now one can say, "Who cares?"

In my Mediterranean town this buried life is a luxury; in this town it is a necessity.

46

31

If time were a road in a crystal hive and one entered the *now* and came out in any *then* — in time of Abelard, let's say, of Caesar, Dionysius or Pisistratus, even — the one thing one would find intact among the resurrected ruins would be the Demon's gift.

A man of this town, my friend William, could love a Joan of Arc. A man in my Mediterranean town could love Jeanne of this town.

The fireflies have told me this.

When the fireflies appear in June, I put out all the lights and watch them throbbing, their lights signaling in the dark. What are they signaling? How? I count their flashes; one, two, three, four, five, then darkness — one, two, three, right through to ten, then darkness. Be calm, be calm. Or is it one, two, three, four, five, then one, two, three answered by one, pause, one and the lights rush to one another?

One firefly comes to rest on the window ledge and with no other light around throbs once... one... one; then one, two, one, two; then one, two, three; its light swells and holds on. It is ivory around the outer edge; it's so brilliant it seems bottomless until my eyes accustom themselves to the brightness and I can see a speck of green, a field of green. The firefly is exhausted, spends the night clinging to my window. In the morning I find it dead, its legs torn off, part of its belly eaten.

32

Just before my friend saw Jeanne again, he began to paint furiously: sketches of landscapes, of the lake, the surrounding hills, a single maple in pastels, charcoal studies of the tree from every angle, and then a canvas of the River Dunbar where it flows into Lake Vernon. He had no patience for portraits, except to try a portrait of Jeanne from a photograph she had left as a book marker in *The Hobbit*. Jeanne never wanted to be photographed. Those paintings my friend could not finish he slashed at with large brushes and turned into plastic movements of anger. Anger, because he had not studied painting earlier, that he could not capture the calm sheen of that peace without boredom, that fine brittle brilliance of the evening by the river when all seemed varnished by the sun just behind the hills. It angered him that he could not remember what Jeanne's face was like.

33

When Jeanne smiled her face radiated happiness. We all felt her happiness — me, William, Elvira, the Irish lady poet — all of us who were to be character witnesses at Bob's trial. No one who ever saw her disliked her, and those who had the need, loved her. It was her radiance, her apparent everlasting youthfulness, for, in spite of the fact that she had seen so much, she smiled at all that she saw as if she were seeing it for the first time. Her smile was a compliment to anyone who made her happy. She smiled, too, with her tight round cheeks, her sharp nose and flaring nostrils, her firefly eyes, her radiant tawny hair, so that often she had the air of a happy female fox.

But it was her happiness that won us all. She was the hope of the world, as my friend William said. Nonetheless, it was that way just the same. She was happiness for the short time she was with us.

"But I'm a rascal, I tell you," she often said to me. "I know how to put it on; eagerness, enthusiasm. I'm a 100 percent American female rascal." She looked away, hummed to herself and then looked back at me and smiled.

"You may know how to put it on," I said, "but it's real, and you can't help it."

34

We asked Loti, who owned the record shop, to be a character witness also. How and why she came to this town is too long to tell. But I know where it began.

At age eighteen, while in a concentration camp, Loti fell in love with a blond Pole named Tadzio. He loved her also and their love kept them alive and sane for that whole year before grey soldiers came to free them and cry at what they saw. Somehow they were separated by the confused events of that time. They wrote to each other, she from Lemburg, he from Warsaw, in a time when they both decided to flee to Paris. Tadzio arrived safely, Loti was stopped at a frontier town and sent back to Lemburg. For six months they wrote love letters, sending them across the frontier with ballet dancers and hockey players who were permitted to travel to Paris. The letters from Loti were too touching for Tadzio and he returned to Warsaw where he was arrested and imprisoned before he could see her. For three years Loti lived, waiting for his release and when it came, it was the springtime of their lives. They were married within a week of Tadzio's release and within a year they were divorced.

Loti often told me, "We people of that time had something awful to hold us together and it was wunnerful," and then added, as she did to all her conversations as farewell, "Come to the store, even if you don't buy. Come to the store to see me."

35

I had seen Jeanne by the river a number of times, and one spring night we talked for a while by the flat stone close to the poplars. She had a troubled look and yet when she smiled there was that happiness. She told me that she had married. "It's working out. It's working out," she said, repeating it twice as she did. Her silken-haired husband had acquired a degree, given up his job as bartender and found a job teaching in the local school. She talked smoothly with a humming sound in her voice. I walked her to the bridge and we talked of Tolkien and *The Little Prince*. Then she said something that was true. "All those books — *Lord of the Rings*, *The Hobbit*, *The Little Prince*, those really joyful books, sad and joyful — there is no sex in those books, is there?" And without waiting for an answer she added, "And yet there is."

As she stepped on to the bridge she said quietly, "Bob has been arrested on drug charges, you know. And just when things seemed to be working out."

I watched her cross the bridge and all the way home I debated with myself whether to tell my friend that Jeanne had been living in this town all the time he thought she was away. Only at the telephone did I become aware of the mosquito bites the size of dimes all up and down my legs. Then I heard my friend's voice saying, "Yes, I know. She's married and it seems to be working out."

36

When thoughts of the Demon's gift are too much with me, I spend an evening with Elvira and Alice Mary Humble sipping local champagne, until Elvira goes to the piano and we sing hymns. Then Alice Mary comes out of her silence, and the gnats disturbed — buzz around each other and about her head, aureoles around aureoles, bringing with them an odor of camphor and decay, as we softly begin to sing:

> *Lead, kindly light, amid the encircling gloom*
> *Lead thou me on; the night is dark and*
> *I am far from home . . .*

Alice Mary's voice, now raucous, now breaking, reedy on the high notes; Elvira, her squared-off hair puffed out and white, looking like Einstein as an old man, nodding profoundly at the piano as she plays.

A glass of champagne would put Alice Mary to sleep and Elvira was left with me shouting:

> *Work for the night is coming,*
> *Work in the glowing sun.*
> *Work till the last beam fadeth,*
> *to shine no more.*

Alice Mary would lift her head from time to time and join us, forgetting the hymns and break out with:

> *Do you ken John Peel*
> *with his prick of steel*
> *and his balls o' brass*
> *and his celluloid ass*
> *Do you ken John Peel.*

She sings in such a soft voice that we ignore her. The champagne finished, mostly by me, I walk home. A foot or so high off the ground at that, past the pumping station, down to the river where the fishing boats are launched and across the bridge that bends slightly to my steps. I sing softly to myself a song I remembered the men in my Mediterranean town singing as they come home on muleback:

When your love's face begins to fade
Throw yourself upon the earth
and start collecting snails.

How lonely this town is, how temporary; the moorings have been torn out . . . the avenues of harm are open. Jeanne understands, I do, William does, the character witnesses do, we all do, except the prosecutor Sewall and the Judge wearing a blue polka-dot bow tie — but then this town has been abandoned to lawyers in their offices above liquor stores, in abandoned stores, shopping centers and colonial houses.

37

The widow's son, in the second year the painter had returned, to my Mediterrean town, came to take lessons, "like learning to dance from the lame," some said. Others came to talk, until one day, while he drank his whiskey, he began to sketch the faces of the men around him as they told their stories. He would look casually at men's faces, then go to a table facing a dark brick wall where he would work for five, fifteen minutes, alone. Then, returning to the group

with a tumbler of whiskey in his hand and a frightened, haunted look, he would listen for a while and
then suddenly return to the table.

The men became used to this and continued
their talk, until he would return again. By noon he
would be dancing and singing around the theater until one o'clock, when the widow would come to put
him to bed for the afternoon, saying, "How beautiful
you are," mockingly, for she had learned to protect
her own feelings by humor. And the master-painter,
in an equally mocking tone said, "Well, you had better make use of me while you can. There isn't much
time left."

38

We'd sit by the river and Jeanne would tell me of
the time she fled our town, confused and angry, with
an orange colored pack on her back. "I guess I loved
this town. I thought it was the most beautiful place
in the world. I loved it. I was told it was honest and
good, the hope of the world. Then they started killing people on the other side of the world. Just to
make them as good and beautiful as us, and they
started killing my friends. I went on marches to stop
it. And they threw brown paper bags that hit me in
the head and shit came down all over my face. "Why
did they do that?" She paused and looked up to the
town above us, then went on, "So I fled and I know,
I know, I wanted to be humiliated."

"In the Bay of Donegal a fishing boat captain or something asked me to come out for a short ride, of a half hour or so," they said. We didn't come back until two days later.

"God, the food was greasy and all those fat men. I'll never forget . . ." She smiled. "You wouldn't believe it. You know, there was a nun waiting for me when I returned. She was sitting on an upturned boat; you wouldn't believe — my mother once wanted me to be a nun."

She looked across the lake to the distant mountains and turned to the town again. After a while she looked at me. "They thought they had all fucked me. But I didn't care. I didn't."

39

Jeanne was a free and easy presence all her own with as much love to give as she was beautiful. She loved like a child, that is, with innocence and complete abandonment, happy that love had come to her like a grace, as if for the first time.

She loved our town that way. When she saw its corruption, and vices, its buried life, for the first time she swore that she would fight to wipe away its egotism and replace it with morality, corruption with honesty, fucking with love-making, insolence with pride in oneself, greediness with generosity, hustlers with beautiful people, meat-eaters with vegetarians, assembly line workers with artisans.

One more effort and our town would be put right.

"How naive," the prosecutor Sewall said.

40

There is a mindless love that, when it comes, it seems to come like death itself, but only once, and leaves no history, just small stories. Manage your joys and manage your sorrows, my friend — *hic hoc*.

41

"I understand this restlessness now that has made me rattle around from state to state and room to room," William said to me one Sunday afternoon.

"I've been a lover looking for someone to love." He still looked grim and in need of solace. I tried to comfort him, "Or it might be that there is a full moon tonight."

"It's been a month of full moons," he said.

"Come on now. There are some things you can't do anything about."

"She's so young and fragile. She's going to get hurt."

"Don't get into that," I said. "It's the old men who are fragile." I had the feeling he wasn't listening and I went on to say, "Anyway if you could sleep with her a week you'd begin to say how tough she was. It's

just your fear that she's rolling in the arms of someone else. It's you who are fragile for the moment."

He wasn't listening, he was looking out across
the lake.

"She is the hope of the world to me. I love her.
I'm not jealous really. It's strange but I'm not jealous
of Bob."

"I know. I know."

"God, what is this thing I have about Jeanne?"

I wanted to tell him not to be hoggish about life.
He had had his turn.

"I never loved like this before."

"I know, I know. You're getting close to forty-
nine; the nines are bad."

"No, I've never loved like . . ."

"One never does. It will pass."

"I writhe in bed."

"I know, I know. The nights are bad."

"I pace from room to room."

"I know."

"It's these Sundays, they're worst of all."

"I know," I said. "*A man is always as happy as
his Sundays.*"

42

One evening when the fireflies were pale against
the fading light I found Jeanne walking slowly across
the bridge towards me. Her face lit up when she saw
me and we sat at the river's edge beneath the poplar

57

trees. The world seemed to shrink as it grew dark; the mountains in the distance disappeared, then the outer edges of the lake were gone; slowly the fishing boats vanished and we were left with the poplars reflected loosely in the dark river light, with the fishermen's voices and the fireflies all around the bridge. Some were in Jeanne's hair like confetti and on her mauve gauze blouse; some in my hair too and we sat there winking at each other in coded lights — one, two, three — pause — one, two, three — pause — a code I could not understand.

"But if you loved each other as you did, why did you leave him last summer?"

There was a silent explosion of fireflies all around her head as she spoke.

"I knew it would die and I preferred to leave with that gentle triumph. And Bob needed me. My husband, Bob, became my reality. He needed me. Love is bullshit . . . sometimes. Your friend . . . I don't know, he became . . . He is something very precious."

The light was gone. The sky just then was filled with firefly sharp lights exploding low in the grass, high in the trees and shooting like stars high above our heads; some throbbing softly, green; others crackling like soundless strings of fire crackers, a few gliding on their own light — opening flashes — as they came towards us, to another world.

43

William grew even more grim. He took to photography to help him paint and began to take piano lessons with Elvira who told him that a good piano stroke began in the buttocks, a fact that most piano teachers ignored, she said. It was no help to him just then when he believed that Jeanne had left to humiliate this town through her own humiliation.

In the evenings I'd see him drive by, Adam, the Newfoundland dog beside him, looking as mournful as his master. Poor Adam, each time he got in the car, had an erection as red as an old lipstick. Often my friend would end up hugging him after he had kicked him for having barked suddenly at a robin or a passing small blue car.

44

Oh, I'm glad you've come and that you've brought your armagnac.

Would you laugh at me if I told you that my friend's spirit at this moment is at the heart of Western man's restlessness? Jesus, excuse me. I'll have some of your armagnac. Excuse me that remark, "Western man," Jesus.

What do I mean by that? Well, it's too complicated and it might not be worth the digging up of words.

You insist?

In exchange for your armagnac, then.

My friend once told me of something that happened to him.

He was coming back from the war with three years of love stored up in him. Somewhere in the West the train stopped at a small town. He got off to get a drink and by the soda pop machine he saw a girl, the loveliest he had seen in three years. They looked at one another and without a word he was kissing her, he had lifted her skirt and his hips were pushing into her cold flanks. He was near exploding when the train began to pull out. He put out his hand. She put out her hand to him and smiled a generous smile.

The image of the girl on that Western station had stay stayed with him through an education, two marriages, several children.

He kept her in his privacy and yearned for her. It was his lyricism. He was restless for her, and became successful in search of her.

How?

Now, I've seen Roman walls in Scotland, Roman baths in Bath and Roman theaters in Budapest and Antioch. What made those men wander around like that, on foot? Why is it really that no Chinese Columbus came looking for us? There is nothing as explosive as the hopefulness of love as we know it. Did Gurdjieff speak of love? This town speaks so much of love, it's obsessed with love, isn't it? And yet to find a bit of genuine love is a breathless surprise. Tyrants in their secret councils speak of moments when whole continents shall hold their breath and wait. There is a tie between love and Imperial dominion. Oh, excuse me. These words are useless.

Your armagnac is good tonight. I'm beginning to talk like Gurdjieff, you say? No, he avoided it like the rest of us; the Romans, the Crusaders, Marco Polo, Columbus, Chinese Gordon — I mean to say, why this restlessness to run off to other people, as if to run away from home? Home is marriage and Jeanne is the Orient. And if you give me another glass, I'll say Jeanne is the Northwest passage and my friend is an imperialist. And once he's conquered her, he'll be off again to seek new profits elsewhere. He must. It's the Demon's gift to the Western world; our restlessness is in our way of loving. If Christ had had a few battalions, he would have been no pacifist. Certainly he was no Christian; you have to have armies to be a Christian. Oh, I'm sorry for that, too. No, it's not the armagnac. It's love — the worm in the apple of the Western world. All love is self love; that's why the first to fall out of love is not hurt; he's almost pleased, isn't he? The other mourns for himself, herself. My friend is mourning for himself. Jeanne was right — all those books that the young love so much — Tolkien, Hesse, Gurdjieff too — there is a world constructed without love, fucking love — excuse me for that — but there is no fucking love and they feel comfortable. And what are we to make of that?

You two seem so happy because you never talk about it.

61

I wish you both peace without boredom and exhilaration without restlessness.

45

I find myself thinking more and more of my Mediterranean town since my gentle friend became so
grim. In my Mediterranean town from the hill they
call the Saracen, I can see the houses strewn down in
the sun like children's blocks and in the distance a
towering volcano where once a philosopher despair-
ing in his old age, threw himself, leaving only a san-
dal in remembrance of the time he spent in the town.
By the time the children and elders learn to live with
one another, he said, it is too late.

There is poverty in my Mediterranean town, the
land is worn out and the people are used.

I find myself thinking more and more of all that
in this town which had a second chance in its hand
but blew it to the winds. Still, such a thing could not
have happened between my friend William and
Jeanne in my Mediterranean town — the land exhausted, men withdraw to families for comfort; such
emotions are too costly.

46

In my Mediterranean town there is an iron cage that
can be assembled from bits and pieces of curved iron

until it is the size of a small room. It is used in cases of violent madness only. There's no need for certification; when the car arrives with the pile of iron bits, curved in sorrow, everyone knows the man is mad, and the bits and pieces are taken into the house and assembled around the mad man. There is no door to the cage. The family cares for him, passing him urinals and plates of thick soup through the bars. And his, their own, insanity is constantly before them. There is not another cage in the town and men must wait their turn to go violently mad.

47

Where have all the young come from in this town who sit leaning on the pillars of the First National Bank and watch?

They speak a language all their own, a vulgar tongue to those who don't understand it, as if to curse the stark reality of this town and those who brought freedom to jungle people while bringing tyranny to their own.

Jeanne's new-found coarseness and vulgarity was part of this and at first disturbed my friend — to hear her say, "My husband, he must get his cock together, my cunt needs filling."

And yet later I found this note he had written.

I'll fill your cunt with joy and happiness. I'll fill it with comfort and love. I'll fill your cunt with

peace and pleasure and exhilaration. I'll fill your
soul with poppies and babies' breath picked from
mine, and in the morning I'll fill your bowl with
Cherrios.

I hope no one from my Mediterranean town
hears this. They would not understand such vulgar,
angry freedom in the time of love and courtship.

48

If you live long enough, everything will happen to
you, simply because things won't come at you in the
same way, as they say. Things won't jump out of trees
like flat stones of light skipping over a pond
stretched tight in the low late summer light; things
will come at you and take the shape of tables and
chairs in the flat kitchen light — if you live long
enough. But memory remains, a seed blown from
mind to mind and place to place, to skip along the
gloss of time, to stretch and break, to settle in the
kitchen light among the tables and the chairs and
waits to bloom.

49

On the first day of the Feast-Day of the Dead the
master painter in my Mediterranean town, would begin his story in this way:

In a far off city of this world, many years ago, I found in the newspapers the description of a terrible murder. At the same time I was reading a book by a man of science in which he said, "All that we see and observe has nothing to do with the movements of planets in space, but with temporal changes caused by the stars and this earth in the flow of time." I felt something shiver in me.

The last place, I figured, a conjunction of the stars and this earth could have caused such events to come together for the third time, I believed, would have been on an ocean liner leaving one of those large cities for the Mediterranean on July 29th, 19... And for this reason I believed that I had offended a power, an intelligence beyond my understanding.

On February 29th of that year I was in England. In a northern city, a young woman left her home to go to evening school. She never returned to her home, where she had lived with her widowed mother. An extensive search did not find her, and only when she had been almost forgotten was her body found and then in conjunction with another murder. On September 5th of that year, the body of a young girl was found in an abandoned house, on a table. Beside her on the floor was the body of the girl missing since February, half-decomposed, her throat cut. These details horrified the city, especially since the two girls were from good families.

In Paris a few years later, my work going poorly, I spent my days in the great library reading the memoirs from beyond the grave by a famous French writer. There I read that he had met a laundress, a lovely young woman who gave him an appointment for the next evening. When he arrived he found the laundress lying dead on the ironing table and, beside her on the floor, the cadaver of another girl, her body half-decomposed and her throat cut. This incident had made a great impression on the writer. It must have, because he recorded the date, September 5, 1784.

Here the painter would turn to the wall and draw with pen and ink the faces of young women with large haunted eyes. He would continue his story the next day.

50

The first year we had our Wednesday night dinners, we began to call my friend the philosopher because of his gentleness, his calmness and resignation before all that happened to him. Not that he was born that way; it was a tranquility he had acquired. He had learned to accommodate to the world. It may have been because he had the tranquility of a painter who looks at the world through half-closed eyes, looking for shadows and for light to help him order the world that lies in his mind. He never raised his voice and he walked deliberately, as if each step he took was the first in a long ramble along a country road he knew well, one he liked very much. It was hard to catch his eye when he walked about this town with never a quick move. His walk was as smooth as his mind that told him, "Either way you're going to suffer . . ."

The absence of Jeanne made his tranquility evaporate, as if by some conjurer's trick.

Jeanne called him a gentleman.

51

A man wrote of my Mediterranean town that anyone who once knew that town and surrounding countryside could never be quite free from the nostalgia for it. My friend was living a nostalgia for Jeanne and would never be quite free from it. As any one who has once known this life and is at the point of death can never be quite free from the nostalgia for it.

52

I remember the night the young came out in the streets crying, "They're killing students!"

There was a madness, a persistent madness in the air, and Jeanne's own madness was born that night when her man was going mad and her friends were sobbing in the streets; thousands were in the streets with candles, chanting: "Stop the killing in Viet Nam." And seemed with one more effort this town would be put right.

Then the old men in spirit — the lawyers and the scientists — came out when all the speeches had been made and all the debating was over. Then the scientist spoke, "As a biochemist, I would like to get back to my work. As much as I might understand the youngs' feelings, I see no point in my discussing a jungle war or the unfortunate death of four young people."

There was a scattered applause.

"The glow is going. It's fading," my friend beside me muttered.

A tired poet who in his youth had been a rebel, who now loved birds and ate meat only because his wife would have left him if he didn't, spoke from notes and told us that once he, too, wanted to destroy; now he understood that if anarchy was not to triumph, the elders must control.

A bearded real estate agent said, "I move that we do nothing. Those who are in charge know more than we do. We must support them."

The scientist had just arrived from his evening nap. He had not marched and was fresh, yet his face twitched; his tongue flicked out from his dry mouth. "The sooner we get back to work, the better it will be."

Someone yawned, seats were beginning to empty, someone moved that nothing be done. The lawyer Sewall seconded the motion. The dead were forgotten.

The scientist brushed the strands of hair across his balding head, straightened his glasses with both hands and with a hunching movement of his shoulders adjusted his jacket, cleared his throat and sat back in his seat.

Behind me I heard a young tearful voice, "These men will always control this town, won't they?"

Outside there was a roar as huge bombers began to take off wearing their frog-like camouflage, and as they made lazy, bored turns to the east, exposed their tender white bellies.

It was soon after that evening Jeanne left with her orange colored pack for her humiliation.

53

The men who built the bridge across the River Dunbar saw the iron world for the first time. They were fortunate. The first look at anything is exhilarating. The bridge is lively because of it. They knew where to put it, just where the river narrows and then widens suddenly into the broad expanses of the lake. We've looked at the town around us through their fresh eyes, my friend, myself and Brian. To live in a time when the first fresh look is tarnished and that whole vision is dying is no comfort.

My friend saw Jeanne just as her own first fresh look at this town was fading. He saw her as happiness for the last time.

54

When men and women are in love they want to tell someone about this first fresh look. "You see, I've seen this lovely sunrise," or "I've heard this enchanting song . . . I've discovered this unique woman. See how the grass looks like velvet in the evening light." There is nothing as common as being in love, and yet love needs to be unique.

Both my friend and Jeanne told me this.

She would come across the bridge and tell me that the nights were worst of all, and she'd begin to rub her nose with the palm of her hand and lightly scratch one cheek and then the other. "The nights are worst of all. I'm so fucking restless. I want your friend to be with me, and me with him. I want him to touch me. And then I think. I'm only three months married and I want it to work! I care for Bob and he needs me and I love him."

And without stopping.

"Do you think . . . ? Can one make a mistake? Do you believe in mistakes?"

"If it concerns only you; you can," I said. "But not with other people, you can't."

"What do you mean?"

"I once drove to another city on an icy cold day." I said. "I shouldn't have done that. I went because I was afraid, twenty miles out I went into a skid, after touching the brakes lightly, hit a snow bank and flipped over in the air. The roof of the car cracked

down on my head . . . I was sure it was my neck crack-
ing. I thought I was dying. The car landed back on its
wheels in deep snow and I was without a scratch.
Going out that day was a mistake. On my own I went
out and an accident occurred. No one else with all
the complexity of a life, took part in that mistake, of
going out to prove I could overcome fear. Who made
the mistake in loving before you married Bob? My
friend, you? Who made the mistake in marrying, you
or Bob? A committee can commit suicide only by a
unanimous vote. You, my friend and Bob — there are
no mistakes, either way, some will be good and some
will be bad, you know that, Jeanne."

"I never loved like this."

"I know, I know."

55

The night that students were killed, Jeanne was in
a fury. She had grabbed a bull-horn to say, "Now
we're going to march on the air base. Keep four
abreast. Don't let them provoke you. Remember,
there are many others in this town with us tonight."

She then had to run to comfort Bob and came
back to find herself on the street with a friend, arrested. When she was released she was at the Federal
building sleeping in its corridors, preventing a raucous Marine from entering.

She cried at the meeting when the biochemist
and the lawyer Sewall carried the motion to do noth-

ing. That was May and in the month of June she was tramping through Ireland and drinking whiskey in pubs from anyone willing to pay for her drink. And then she traveled to the ancient cities near my Mediterranean town.

The jungle war gave Jeanne a store of love, as if she saw something she cherished being destroyed and she had to find someone to give it to quickly. I often thought in those days that the thing we call history had a greater effect on all our lives than did any mindless toilet training of our childhood.

56

Adam, William's Newfoundland dog, loved to ride in back of the car and during those grim days each time he jumped in the back seat, he spread his haunches to expose a lipstick red erection. He did not want to be left alone in that time and all my friend had to do was to leave a car window half open and he'd find Adam in the back, his tongue happily hanging out until my friend took to beating him, throwing shoes and plates at him, because he had scratched a fender trying to get into the car. It always ended — five or ten minutes later — with my friend hugging the cowering dog. "What are we to do, Adam? Have patience with me."

Adam did not have command of a large vocabulary and soon began to chase small blue cars, the color and size of my friend's last wife's car.

Jeanne came to love this town for the harm it was doing to itself — out of protectiveness really — much as old men fall in love with young girls.

One day while walking in the bohemian quarter of this town I saw a man about my age, slim and straight, with a small soft white beard. Clinging to his arm was a wide-eyed girl of about twenty. She walked beside him proudly. She had eyes for no one but him. He looked straight ahead with a boyish smile on his face. The girl suddenly turned on her toe, her hair whirling with her, and she kissed him full on the lips and walked with him this way for a few steps. Just then I caught his eye, and he mine, and when the girl whirled back in step, he lowered his eyes from mine and blushed.

58

It was a luminous afternoon. Where I like to walk the air around the stones that jut out over the river was thick with mosquitoes and deer flies. I sat watching the insects skimming the water, the purple swallows swooping down from time to time, their wing tips flicking up drops of water from the still river, and the perch leaping out of their water into our world, sending ripples towards me. I constantly slapped my arms, my legs, and back. I crushed a deer fly, a perfect triangle with a snout nose. One bit me and my thigh began to swell. I watched the bridge, and slapped without thinking or looking at the black insect on my bare leg. I stunned it and it lay in my lap, a black sunflower seed writhing, its long antennas uncoordinated, swaying out of rhythm; its legs curling and uncurling, the small praying-mantis head gasping for breath, trying to turn over its orange belly from the sun. I tried to turn it over and once I do so, but its writhing legs up-ended it again. I saw its orange belly throb and then it was still. Its antenna curled until a gust of wind blew it out to the river. It was a firefly. There was a sudden splash, the still water broke, the firefly was gone, sending ripples ever widening towards me.

59

I don't know how William made contact with Jeanne again or whether it was she who called, although I could never believe it was she. She never looked back, and if the past was to catch up to her it had to run ahead to catch her eye. I do know this. One Sunday afternoon my friend had just come back from a week's trip to the city. He looked grey, his eyes were shining and this gentle friend of mine looked as if he could kick me in the shins just out of nastiness. When I saw him on Monday he was radiant, as if some light within him had been turned on. He smiled, his teeth were bright and sound. His eyes laughed and shone

74

a clear blue-white. He might have hugged me if he were a more demonstrative man. He was a boy embarrassed.

"Hey," he said to me, "I'm going to ask you something, and if you can't do it, just tell me."

I nodded.

"Can you let me have your place; I know you're not there after ten. I just don't want to be with Jeanne at . . ."

"Sure, I only have one key but, come on, I'll go have a key made up."

It was a light aluminum blue key. And my friend still carries it on his key chain.

60

The second great war had left the lawyer Sewall exhilarated because he had liberated a whole continent and experienced the extremes of the sense of dying in a minor skirmish — not far from my Mediterranean town — and then the relief of coming out alive where others died, and the astonishment that a chocolate bar — a simple chocolate bar — produced in this town with so little effort could buy him so much pleasure. It was a lesson imbedded in his mind. This town, his town was number one, this flag was the symbol and the knowledge — not that others were inferior but that he belonged to a people who were better. He had the taste of sweet chocolate in his mouth to prove it.

Soon after the great war the lawyer Sewall was married in a hidden field to which the guests had to walk from a back country road, up a cow path beneath a low row of maples and pine and on to the field, wind swept, overlooking this town, the lake, and the mountains beyond. It was breath-taking to burst out onto that field and see the minister softly pronouncing the sermon while the bride's frock blew in the wind. He was married while still in college. One of the first things he did was to build a house on the site where they were married. It was on that site that he had "sired," as he said, his children and created his buried life.

61

In my old house on loan to me for a monthly fee, the walls are lived in; chipmunks: red squirrels, rats for all I know. I've never seen them, although at night I hear the muffled sounds within the walls beside my ear — a scraping, a gnawing, a sighing, snoring, little cries of pleasure, gentle breathing. Sometimes when I'm awakened late into the soundless night, when my room is like a tomb, I hear within the walls the sound of a head thumping close to my ear and an elbow of the departed soul, the dead that turn over in the walls. In the morning between sleep and wakefulness I think of my friend and Jeanne and how they once slept in this room, and my bed seems as deep and heaving as the sea.

62

In my Mediterranean town the cobblestones are loose; the clock in the hooded towers of the Mother Church is stopped at six although it still rings the hour, the half and the quarter hour. The stones from which the town is built have been used over and over again; now for homes, then for temples, and again for churches, paving stones and wells, so that at the bottom of a well or an attic patio, one finds a stone once part of a temple or pyramid of an ancient people.

Such things would not have happened in my Mediterranean town where most things happen to one once, and if one misses it, God help you. Most men love once, the roads are cobblestoned but once, the church is built but once. And only when the very seeds of memory are dead are the temple stones used to build a church or well.

Jeanne at twenty-three had lived a dozen lives of anyone in my Mediterranean town, and because of her unawareness of her own gluttony for life, had harmed and transformed everyone she touched. She had shaken loose her high school teacher from his classes, and he went to live in the woods where he became a good farmer. A community college unhappy poet was killed when he crashed into a brick wall while going to her one frozen night.

With Bob, her husband, she had been married only three months when he was arrested on the charge of selling cocain.

It was known by all, the thirty-four lawyers, the six judges in this town, that the prosecutor Sewall had bargained with a witness who was a thief and smuggler, telling him, "I'll get you three and in one a parole instead of twenty years and no parole — if you turn state's evidence. We want everyone up and down this line."

Bob had kept a package for the thief behind the counter of the bar, a year ago when there was the madness in the air because of the distant war.

63

Brian Davis came back from India on a hot muggy day without the essence or the perfection he had gone to look for, although he did come back wearing a yellow toga and with an air of tranquillity that lasted about two weeks.

When he heard of those villians who had stolen and cheated in the highest places, and that a man he scorned had been made Chief Executive of where he worked, he quickly forgot the essence and perfection he had gone to India to find, and said he found the truth in a phrase he repeated often — "We're all treading water." He lived contented with Chris for a month, discovering the pleasures of, as he said "fucking with someone you like." But when Chris demanded marriage, his body refused. His left leg the night before the wedding became paralyzed and Chris refused to marry him for fear he might become impotent. And Brian began again his furious round of women, at the heart of which, I believe, was love itself.

Brian was like the man who wished to maintain the headiness of a wine — as he sensed the love of a woman fading, he sought another, and that new emotion sustained him until this, too, began to fade, "to go out of focus," he said. Panic would set in he and looked for the woman "beyond the hill," and then another, until he found a high-pitched stability, the balance of one more drink that keeps a drunk exhilarated for a month — so as not to lose the miraculous.

64

Love demands a clear day in the heart. I alone could walk with Jeanne along the river on those warm grey days. She'd talk to me in her steady voice, as if to herself, while she rubbed her nose with her open palm, and from time to time scratched her cheek. "Bob is really taking it great. I don't know how he does it. It's been hanging over his head now for months and he just says, 'Fuck it.' They can give him fifteen years. We talked about it. Even if he gets three years, 'You'll be free,' he says. The others who were in on it, they did the real pushing. They got three years. And the lawyer was optimistic. Now he is down, because Bob has no state's evidence to turn. He keeps telling Bob, 'We'll wait until the case gets stale,' and Bob just says, 'Fuck it.' "

She rubbed her nose and was silent. Then she looked at me. "This morning your friend called. We were in bed. I rolled over and picked up the phone. Bob was still asleep. We talked. His voice troubled me. Then Bob came awake and he had an erection. I'd never seen his cock like that, and he was in me. I leaned over the edge of the bed so your friend wouldn't hear his breathing."

"You're still too much with me," your friend said.

"And Bob was working away behind me.

" 'Love is trust,' your friend was saying."

"Love is sharing," I answered back.

"I'm a manipulating bitch, hey?" she laughed.

I didn't say a thing.

"I'm a rascal. And I care deeply for my Bob, and I love your gentle friend."

The hills that day looked particularly indifferent across the lake, except for the darkness among the trees.

65

One evening, soon after, I met my friend by the river. He was smiling and so happy that he made little snoring sounds as he rushed to tell me, "I called

Jeanne this morning," and then he went on to say that her voice was soft and tender, full of love. "She must have just awakened. I know that innocence in her morning voice, when Jeanne's being is clear and all her own."

"How is she really?"

"My voice troubled her. I know that. And I told her, '*you* are too much with me.' She made a humming sound I know so well.

" 'Love is trust,' I told her."

" 'Love is sharing,' she said, and her voice took on that tender distractedness I know so well, and she kept repeating, 'I love you, I love you,' as if she were out of breath."

The hills looked as indifferent as ever that evening, except for the one or two late fireflies that winked at us in the darkness. I felt like those bleak spaces between the trees across the lake.

66

Bob's lawyer often had lunch at the Drake club with the prosecutor Sewall and Judge Elliot where in conversations over coffee they attributed the chaos and the poverty of my Mediterranean town to the excessive respect for family life. "It's the reason they are so backward — no sense of market value." They all agreed.

Bob's lawyer was considered good, not because he lunched with these two men, but because he never lost a case, it was said. He had helped the prosecutor Sewall be elected. He was a highly active attorney "which was another way of saying that he knew the ways of pulling the right strings for the benefit of everyone." If some were astonished by the fees he charged, he simply said, "Would it be more to his benefit to sit three years in jail?"

Bob had been left $5,000 a year before by an aunt who died in an automobile accident. It was one of the first things the lawyer found out in his exploratory talks with Bob. He assured Bob that would be enough. But even the court guard knew that the case would be drawn out, "just to scare the shit out of the kid." The lawyer had little to do. Bob would have been smarter to plead guilty and throw himself on the mercy of the court. The lawyer knew there was little or nothing to do, and took the money anyway. I heard this from the court guard who having listened to lawyers for ten years had come to the conclusion, "The laws are made by lawyers for lawyers."

67

At one of our first dinners together after Brian's return, my friend William seemed to have a fever. His eyes were tearless and shining. From a distance he seemed a healthy rose, yet even at the table I could tell that he was in a constant state of blushing. When he crossed his legs I could see by the pulsating of his leg in mid-air that his heart was beating rapidly.

Brian spoke of India disdainfully, of the appalling poverty that was an embarrassment to him. "How can there be wisdom or perfection in a country where people are treated like vermin. I've seen vultures pulling out the entrails of dead women, right out of their cunts. There is no wisdom in this. They have put fantasies, the miraculous, in their temples and live in squalid reality; they have no dreams. And they come here to teach us tranquility." Then he looked at William who was smiling with his luminous eyes and said to him, "One thing I learned; no one in this town is interested in India or my trip there. Nothing happened here since I left, it seems."

At the end of the meal, with the last cupful of champagne we had brought to celebrate Brian's return, William asked for a cigarette as dessert. As he sipped the remains of his champagne he inhaled, as if he had been smoking all his life instead of just a few weeks. He smiled happily. "Jeanne's coming back, you know," he said to Brian, "and that's no small change."

Brian looked at my friend almost angrily. "That jock! She's just another girl basketball player."

Love is a promise, love is a hope, love is hope of growing better to perfection, love is a willingness to sacrifice, love is an expectation that death will be conquered. Love is a desire to unite and be one, an essence, a uniqueness, love has no past, love has no seed, only a flower. Love is a womb looking for a seed. Love is a child with the first knowledge of death. Love is perfection in innocence. Love is joyous but has no sense of humor. Love is energy.

"Try laughing when you're coming," Brian says. Love is a banality. Have a banality then. How to live with it is heavy on our hearts.

68

Those nights when I could not sleep, and they became more and more frequent now, I walked through this town from bar to bar with such names as Happy Herbie's, Brodi's, Big Sister, The Cosmopolitan, the College Inn, the Sweet Egg. Those summer nights the bars were crowded with the young standing belly to belly, drinking anything liquid, until the sweat from their bodies mingled with damp sawdust and the sourness of beer and wine. Just to breathe gave one a rancid headiness. There was a hurried friendliness in the air which came from being twenty and afraid of being left alone that made everyone drink cup after cup, or leave, until those who were left fucked in the dark corners, and still later on the rickety brown tables to the uproarous clapping of onlookers while two men continued playing snooker around the green pool table.

I caught the eye of one girl pinned in that way to a table by a hairy-backed male, and the pain I saw there was immense. The vices of the aristocrats of my Mediterranean town have come down to everyone in this town: the lawyer Sewall whom I often saw at

Happy Herbie's in his button-down shirt, his raincoat folded neatly over his lap as he watched the nude dancer making love to her finger over and over again; the old who came looking for shadows of love upon the wall; the young out of fear of going home alone, as they say.

The bars were bunkers in the night then. A wide robin's egg blue-eyed girl said one night, "There's a terrible war going on outside and the enemy is advancing knee deep in blood, coming to bring just retribution."

If I were young again and in this town, I'd cut my throat, I think. I never felt more resigned to being old. But then it might be nature's way of preparing one to leave this town.

69

Can you both understand that I came to love Jeanne and that she loved me with her great store of child-like love? There was nothing "gutsy," as she said, between us. Oh, she would have given herself and I would have taken her as a compliment, but I had no need for or desire to. I think she understood that; because of it, I came to know her best of all. I don't know why you want to understand her. You both read Gurdjieff. You both believe in him.

What was she like?

Jeanne had not been raped by a drunken uncle, nor had she loved her father nakedly — two sources so many pallid men return to, to explain a woman's free spirit. And that is what Jeanne was then, a free spirit about to be subdued. She simply had all the attributes to demand much of this town, and life around her confirmed in her mind this right. She had the cunning ability to become the best of what one was looking for. As a young girl she was the joy of football players; she was all animal spirit, playful, graceful, unthinking. "A puppy in the snow," she said. She hated the smell of books then, or those who smelled of books. She made sullen athletes joyful, just to see the counterparts of their own bodies in a girl. Yet, with the help of a high school teacher, when she discovered the pleasure of books, she outdistanced him in his learning, took the best from him and gave more. She became like those she was with: with a drunken poet-singer in Ireland she became a drunk herself, drinking great quantities of whiskey before the day was done, giving him lines of poetry he would turn into songs and loving him and his male accompanist.

Jeanne was no chameleon in this. She brought a harmony to people she was with, for better or for worse. She was loved for it and told that she was a great talent, a beauty, a joy of love, an intelligence.

It was understandable then, if she thought she could put a stop to the jungle war and that in the end, when people threw bags of excrement at her as she marched in protest, that all the proverbs she lived by, which in a way held her together, became meaningless — crumbled. No one had ever hated her and those who needed to, loved her. No, it was not a quirk in her toilet training. She came from a modest family that loved her.

You've read Gurdjieff who tells us that abstraction controls our actions. Jeanne simply loved the world that loved her, and anyone who touched her, she touched in return.

She once talked to me about a poet from my Mediterranean town, telling me that if he had been from our town he would be great — but since he was from a forgotten place, well . . . And then she added, "But then, literature is tied to politics and power too, eh?"

"You've a good head," I said to her, "and it is going to get better, if you have patience with it."

"I know, I know. But sometimes I'm in such a fucking hurry."

"You're beautiful inside and out," I told her.

"You're a healthy old man. But I am not what you think I am. It's just you, not me. You want to see things in me. Don't look at the shadows. Look at me, I am just a hundred percent American female rascal."

And there it was. She was unaware of her gifts, even to her graceful swimming or her writing. She was good at everything she tried and seemed to be waiting to discover the thing she would excell in.

Jeanne often brought me poems she had written the night before, and one day, without explanation, she gave me this to read:

I slipped calmly out of bed that morning. How frightened I suddenly became. I remember trying to make a list of the songs I heard on the radio that morning, telling myself which I'd buy when I was working and I had money of my own. I took my embroidery and the Hobbits — something for my hands, and something for my mind. I fed the cats and remembered I was not to eat. I left the house, telling my mother I was going to the city for the weekend. At one moment I was calm, the next frightened; how far from peace I was and what reason had I to expect I would ever be at peace? I just felt like lying down and weeping with pain. I felt the responsibility for the two bright blue eyes I felt in me. I wanted to lie down but I continued on my way, and would anyone notice me for anything other than a young woman of twenty, almost twenty-one, a rascal, hurrying to catch a bus? I felt a love for my town suddenly as I left, as I felt a love for the inexplicable death I carried in me.

The ride was interminable — yet I did easily what I could never do before; I sat still, not moving or thinking. Just feeling a terror deep within me, a darkness cold and silent, deeper than anything I had ever known. Life is frightening, but I'm not going to give it up yet.

I hated death just then, because it was cold and detached as I wanted to be and was not. I felt nothing for the one whose death was at the end of the bus ride. It was someone else's problem now. I had placed myself in the way of the machinery. I would just drift in a willful passivity. I didn't even think what it would be like — the first time in the big city, to travel uptown. "Take a cab," someone had told me and I did.

That day I learned the subtle fragrance of death while waiting, well-behaved, in a grey-tiled room, the stiff camisole cold on my naked body, my thighs wet, and I with a bottomless source of anguish, eager to speak, yet outwardly indifferent. I learned death's weapons then: coldness, darkness, chaos. I trembled, grey and weak, listening to the sound my thighs made as they opened and broke apart in their wetness. I grew hot and excited, eager for talk, for comfort, and no one there but fear and death. Never had I felt so alone, not even on the long ride home.

When she saw that I had finished reading, she said to me, "I wanted to remember that, and added, "It sounds gutsy now, doesn't it?"

"No," I said, "no, not at all."

Brian often found Loti, who was to be our fifth character witness, drifting in a rubber dinghy, singing German love songs close to the landing by his house.

Two weeks before Bob's trial, Brian received a long distance call from Loti saying that she had decided to end her life. Before he could say a word she had hung up. The next day he received another call from her and she talked about the weather, the loveliness of the lake. "It's such a wunnerful day . . ." and hung up again. She called every day for a week in this way. When the credit card expenses started coming in, Brian knew she meant it.

She was staying at the best hotels, had rented cars with chauffeurs, flying each night to different resort areas. She bought gowns, frequented esthetic beauty salons where one facial had cost her $126; a meal that same evening had cost her $250.

During one call, Brian had exhausted all his arguments. "We love you, please don't do it. You might change your mind. And there's Bob's trial. You must be a character witness. We need you!"

"I really don't care about the trial. It is so small a thing, you know. That is the difficulty though. I really don't care what happens to him. I don't care about anything, that's why . . . the lake looks so beautiful to me . . ."

Brian stopped talking and listened to her as she said the business was going badly. "How can I compete with those discount houses? And I'm so bored. I am bored! No stranger can come into my life. There is no foam in my life; the lake is calm and doesn't care either — no foam."

"It's your life, Loti. If there is anything I can do to help . . ."

She was silent, then Brian heard the line go dead. She called again the next day and described the view from her window. "It's warm and wunnerful."

He didn't hear from her again until the day before Bob's trial. "I just wanted to tell you, Brian. I am going to do it today. It is annuder wunnerful day, you know."

The next day in the southern part of the lake, the police found an inflated rubber dinghy, one paddle, all her clothes and her two credit cards. Two weeks later her body, so mutilated by the fish, the water, and time that no one could recognize it, floated up near the oil docks.

Brian and I were the only two at her funeral. Her husband had been taken to a psychiatric hospital. Brian rented a pickup truck and brought her body to the cemetery at the bend in the river. The grave diggers did the rest. Brian and I waited until the ground was covered and the grave diggers had put their tools in a wheel barrel. When they were out of sight Brian said, "OK, we can go now."

Only when we were in the pickup truck did he tell me that Loti had once told him she had nightmares about cremation.

How far my Mediterranean town seemed to me just then.

72

The Holy Field, the cemetery in my Mediterranean town, has the best houses there, built for the future, the loveliest gardens shaded by tall cypresses and tawny eucalyptus trees. The neat alleys of tombstones with the enameled pictures of the dead stare out of the past — stubbornly. On the high ground where the rich are buried are fine sculptures: a bronze old man holding a lantern looking for the child that is buried just beneath him; a stone that seems to come out of the earth is carved into a woman disappearing into a cave followed by her husband five years later. The dates explain all this. The past belongs to my Mediterranean town like an anchor.

This town where I live now believed that the future belonged to it and used the past to make the future. Certainly, they seemed to learn so little from the past — my friend William and Jeanne. He was pressed by what he was to do. Jeanne all her life thought of what was to be. They had no cemetery to anchor them down and they could fly beyond their minds. Understanding them was in the future, not in the past.

73

In my Mediterranean town there are two sisters, virgin old maids who once were beautiful young girls. In the summer evening they sit on the balcony overlooking their narrow street and eat hot snails from a large aluminum pot. The white haired sister dips her hands into the pot, taps the red sauce out of a snail, with a pin pulls the snail out of its shell, tips back her head and drops it into her mouth laughingly. Then she sucks the sauce out of the shell licking the corners. The younger sister still has solid white teeth, They throw the shells over the balcony and into the street.

From time to time they wipe their hands on their black mourning dresses and say another prayer for the martyrs of Mexico of 1935 as once the archpriest had told them to.

74

The prosecuting lawyer Sewall had become obsessed with the ultimate orgasm. The ultimate woman or the ultimate situation which could produce this extraordinary spasm was unimportant to him. He devised countless entanglements which included mirrors, knotted silken cords, mind narrowing, capillary expanding legal drugs. We knew this through Brian who frequented one of the women who serviced the lawyer in such things, a woman the lawyer soon became bored with.

My friend William's search for the miraculous was a flight from boredom in a different direction.

In that time of Jeanne he described his evenings with his first wife. They often sat eating supper in a wordless room, she listening to the news from an ear plug, he mechanically chewing on the liver she had cooked for him to a turn. If he said, "I saw . . ." and then hesitated for a moment, she filled in "Arthur," as if she were plugged into his mind and not to her radio. That she could fill in his unspoken words after three years of marriage disturbed him. Were there no obscure corners to their conversation as there were no obscure corners in their love making? Every crevice of their minds had been lighted by a flat frontal light, as had their bodies.

Everything was boring. How could he tell her this? This kind woman who took care of him. Instead he withdrew into silence, reading, barricading himself behind a row of books, his work and a screen of pipe smoke. He let her wash his socks and underwear, make the bed and prepare hearty suppers.

Only at work did he come to life, aggressive and friendly. At home he became more and more passive, answering all her queries with a calm, "Yes" or "No" or at best "Perhaps."

On the other side of every human vice if one could turn it over like a heavy coin, I'm sure you'd find the face of boredom. Much of my friend's gentleness came from the great effort he had to make to overcome the waves of boredom.

75

Even the most common of men when he dies leaves the feeling for those who knew him, even briefly, that he was unique and that one like him will never be seen again. A priest in my Mediterranean town said this once from a pulpit carved by a seventeenth-century master whose cherubs were crumbling.

Now I find myself thinking, "Even the most common of love leaves the feeling for those who knew it, even briefly, that it was unique and that one just like it will never be seen again."

One night the fireflies were diminished in numbers. On the branch of an alder I saw a light throb once, twice, then a second of darkness and again the throb of light, once, twice. From the other end of the branch another light throbbed once, a second after; it seemed like an answer. I didn't think much of it because soon after, both lights stopped throbbing.

I saw the process repeated, but this time the two flashes of light from one of the branches was answered by a firefly that I could see on the window ledge. It flashed once, then darkness, and I saw the dark firefly come sailing down from the tree and quickly mount the other. They remained that way for a long time in darkness.

My eyes and mind accustomed to the darkness, I saw this repeated several times. Then I saw a firefly, slightly bigger than the other, flash once in answer to the throbbing light just above. again the firefly came sailing down. As it landed like an awkward duck, the waiting firefly swerved and seized it by the thread-like neck and began eating its gasping body feebly throbbing a green-white light in the night. When only the praying-mantis head and hair-thin legs were left, the killer fly's light began to throb again in answer to the lights above. This time a firefly sailed down and quickly mounted the killer fly and they both were motionless in the dark.

"Life is full of surprises," Jeanne often said.

76

After the first dinner, soon after his return from India, Brian never tired of repeating, "No sooner am I away than you think of tying yourself up with some jock of a kid. Good thing she's married." He began jokingly. But each time he said it his anger grew. Those first few dinners he harrassed William with comments filled with an inordinate anger, an anger too great for its sources.

"You know I'm the king's taster. I'm the lure for the women, who come around like minnows to the net."

William paid no attention. He smiled and went on eating.

"Why is it that we no longer talk about the God Damn War?" I said, trying to change the subject.

"No one cares anymore," Brian said and looking at my friend as if to provoke him. "You know I've protected you for six years now, from your lyricism. If it weren't for me you'd have been married every time you felt your lyricism for a woman. And you'd have a whole menagerie of animals to look after."

My friend smiled and lowered his eyes.

"You're becoming a mushroom and if I don't get you out of it no one will."

And this he did. He told Debrah about Jeanne and my friend William.

Now Debrah had a shrew's tongue and couldn't help telling Nancy who loved William very much, that "he is sleeping with a young basketball player and he is thinking of going off with her."

"But his heart is in this town, he told me that," Nancy said.

"Yeah," Debrah snickered, "his heart may be in this town but he doesn't know the exact address."

77

Years later there was a memorial parade for those students killed because of the jungle war.

We gathered under the old blue pines, about fifty of us. We waited and talked about automobiles.

The young in evening gowns and dark suits on their way to a dance looked at us and wondered, A few others came and joined us until a tall red-headed man gave us each a blunt sperm-white candle. We were about sixty now, whereas three years before we had been 3,000. In the fading light we could hear a popular tune: "Down by the levee, in my Chevy the boys were drinking whiskey and rye . . ."

We passed a theater where a vaudeville show was being presented. A serious clown in evening clothes, his face white and nose bright as a red light, twirled his bamboo cane at us as we passed. Sullen police in the streets watched over us, until we all arrived before a recently-planted spruce tree with cables to keep it straight. A minister in blue jeans spoke of the madness of the war in heart-felt tones while the dance tunes and theater voices came to us from open windows, and our candles burned brightly in the night.

Neither Jeanne, nor William, nor Brian, nor the character witnesses were there. I only caught a glimpse of the lady Irish poet who came to cry, as she did at all weddings, baptisms and funerals:

> I cut my hand
> and the drop
> in the glass
> of water
> swells
> to a perfect flower.
> Oh Vietnam,

thus you are buried
in roses.

78

Married just two months, Jeanne, who loved her husband Bob, called my friend William each day at 10:15 or so to arrange to see him and in the afternoon lay naked, happily, with him and made love until late in the afternoon while her husband was at work.

This would never have happened in my Mediterranean town. It would never have happened that a man, as old as my friend and a girl as young as Jeanne, could have had the avenues of love opened to them. It was painfully — and I can't think of another word — painfully soaring for them, like falling off a high place in each others arms. It was unheard of.

"My friends would freak out," Jeanne told him.

"My friends would think me an old fool," William told Jeanne.

And yet there they were, falling to the depths of the center of my borrowed bed.

In my Mediterranean town their bowels would have been cut out, their heads stoned and their bodies left as carrion for the dogs.

In this town their love was permitted to roll out, before all the character witnesses' eyes, as if we were all indifferent and paralyzed by the lack of principle or God, hypnotized by the capabilities of the human heart when all the horizons were open to our minds. But, then, all streets in this town lead only to the sky.

79

In his delirium my friend said, he sucked Jeanne's salty as a sea urchin. "Oh, the center of sweetness was the color of pink poppies in sunlight with its dark seed hole in its center. All around was a labyrinth of petals, alive as mussels in clear pure water. I breathed life and sucked among the dry sunlit sea-weed — feeling with my tongue for the sea flesh I scented there. While she offered her sea urchin as if it were a cat's chin to be scratched and as I stroked her, she raised her haunches and arched her back ... Why is it that all the attributes of lovemaking-cunts, cocks, sperm, the accommodating juices — all smell of the sea?"

80

In old age or late summer, a man reflects upon those things he saw in much confusion in early spring.

In my Mediterranean town, an old priest used to take the children into the wine cellar with its thick white-washed walls where he kept six barrels (round as whales) of fermenting wine, the harvest of his five acres of patrimony.

He'd put his finger to his lips, "Shhhh, Shhhhh, listen," he would say. "Come with me and listen." And took them down the narrow circular stairs that led to the cellar. The air was filled with humming that grew louder and louder until the thick walls began to vibrate. As they walked down, the air became warmer, the humming increased even more, until they were before the six barrels, hot as bread just out of the oven.

"Put your hands on them, feel how warm they are and listen. Listen, the wine is singing."

81

The summer Jeanne spent away from my friend William she met a sixty-five year old glassblower who told her he had been waiting for her for ten years.

He had first seen her, he said, on the platform of a railroad station, standing by a soda pop machine, Jeanne told me. "She had eyes as soft and wild as moths."

The eyes had stayed with him through an education, a marriage, a divorce, a retreat to a narrow dark valley where he began to blow glass heated in furnaces he had built himself. Jeanne met him while hitchhiking and was so taken by him that she visited his farm and spent a month watching while he worked, staring into the raucous volcano of a furnace, his fingers cunningly twirling the rod deep into the heat of the furnace with all the patience of an old man who had more to give the furnace than he wanted or needed from it.

"What became of him?" I asked Jeanne.

"Who?"

"The old man."

"Which old man?"

"The glassblower,"

"The sixty-five year old glassblower and the twenty-two year old princess were married and we lived happily ever after," she said.

"Happily ever after."

82

There is a point of violence everyone faces from time to time, a point at which one must choose between violence and the loss of those delicate mysteries that hold a man together, as if the sources of courage are in the taboos of a town.

In my Mediterranean town a young boy fell in love with a girl of sixteen who lived on the same street as he. His love had developed slowly, but nonetheless surely. The girl's parents were opposed to their marriage at first, but as the boy demonstrated that he was serious — he had a job as a vendor of cloth, they became resigned to the engagement. The boy and the girl saw each other every day, always in the presence of someone of the family. Their physical contact was limited to holding hands, to their cheeks brushing, or his hand touching lightly her hip or breast, as if by accident.

Such encounters only made them wish for an even earlier marriage than their parents had proposed. But he had his military service ahead of him, so they waited.

In the early summer the young couple and their parents went to the seashore where, after a meal, the young couple wandered off to a cove whose sand was so warm and dry that their bodies ignited with the sudden discovery of the power of their feelings. No sooner had the young man erupted wildly within his woman, that the horror of what had happened entered his mind. If she had permitted him to make love to her, then there must have been someone before him.

The girl noted his grimness at the moment but, because she had no experience in such matters, thought it was part of the act of love.

The next days began a torment for the young girl. Each time they met he calmly but persistently wanted to know if there had been someone before him. All her insistence that there had been no one else could not dissuade him. He bombarded her with, "You must tell me who it was. Who was it?"

Her tears and cries of "But there has been no one. You're the first man I've ever loved, who's ever touched me," such phrases simply made the young man silent. And when he spoke, his face white, the question was again, "Who was it?"

To settle the question the young girl consented to visit a doctor. She was examined and after two days of waiting they both climbed the three flights of stairs to the old doctor's office while the mother waited below.

The doctor arranged the papers on his desk, set a pen to the right, slid an old ink well to the left, then opened his palms and said, "The scar is not recent and you really can't tell about these things. You can't tell about these things. You know."

The young man heard nothing but the phrase, "The scar is not recent," which reached him as if it were a blow. He took the young girl gently by the arm and on the landing between the third and second floor asked her, "Who was it?"

"No one! No one! You're the only . . ."

He slapped her and threw her against the wall and as she sank to the steps he took a revolver from his pocket and fired once just below the stomach and squarely between the legs. Then he turned the gun upon himself pointed to his ribs, just below the heart, and fired.

A blind man told me this one summer in an abandoned theater in my Mediterranean town where old scars are obscenities.

83

The soft steady rains had brought out the worms. The young were hunting for night crawlers in the cemetery again. I could see their lights winking across the river among the tomb stones. At my feet was a worm the thickness of my small finger, one end wrinkled like a baby just born, as yet unfolded. It writhed slowly and blindly, its end just off the ground. Its head bandaged in wrinkled grooves lifted up and I saw its mouth puckering and opening as if looking at me. A one-eyed worm. The head or tail fell to the ground, it turned and, finding a hole, slowly penetrated the earth and disappeared in the folds of the ground.

The Demon's gift, I'm sure, is sent by the one-eyed worm.

84

Jeanne's husband Bob had to appear in court a second time in mid-summer. The trial began among the lawyers who knew each other as friends and colleagues.

The courtroom itself was a large room with high ceilings; the seats were pews; the judge's bench an altar; and Judge Elliot, whose father had been a furrier, sat behind it wearing a blue polka-dot tie as large as a Monarch butterfly underneath his black robes. He had the air of a priest without belief, not quite resigned to his lack of faith.

Judge Elliot was forty-nine, unmarried and lived on the wealth accumulated by his father who, having made a fortune in the fur trade, had risen in the realm of politics to the rank of chief accountant. He had a reverence for this town, as only those who have come despised and have risen to a place of esteem, can have. He revered this town, so much so that as a boy of twenty he had changed his ancient name to Elliot and never told, not even to his son, Judge Elliot, what that old name had been.

He had left this attitude of reverence to his son along with a good education, excellent connections. The judge himself developed an impatience with women, and a preference for luxury. He had a rambling home on the lake, two boats, a maid and an Imperial which he traded in every other year, as good business sense dictated. The car was always the same color, gold, although Bob called it "shit brown" with its judge's plaque and "Elliot l" as a license plate.

In assembling the character witnesses, Jeanne's husband's lawyer wanted ten in all. Those who had been chosen were Elvira, Alice Mary, the lady Irish poet, Debrah, a priest and my friend William.

William said though, he had to think about it. He told me, "I might be prejudiced in the case." The lawyer asked for more time to assemble at least five more. His object was, he said, to show that Jeanne's husband was a stable member of the community now, married to a lovely, intelligent woman. William knew Judge Elliot and insisted that Jeanne never come to court, nor Debrah.

"The old women, the lady Irish poet, are OK. But don't bring lovely women to his court. Judge Elliot is not very bright and won't understand that he would convict Jeanne's husband because of her beauty."

The appearance in court lasted about ten minutes. The judge said he would be on vacation for two weeks and then Bob's lawyer said he would be gone the third week. The trial was postponed to the end of August.

Bob simply said, "Fuck it," and went about his living and waited.

85

I learned a great deal about my friend William that summer, no doubt because to be in love is to willingly look to and accept insanity. He talked to himself aloud. I could see his lips moving as he walked about the town frowning. He talked to himself in my presence.

My friend had moved from what many simple people would call success to success, and yet that summer he asked me, "Do you feel like a failure? I mean do you think your life has been a success?"

I knew he was asking of his own life, so I said, "My mother thought I was a success. She often said I had a head of gold because I could read Latin. My father did so too, because I had a high forehead, although he was a little disappointed that I didn't make more money."

"Oh, but it's easy to make money," my friend said, "nowadays . . ."

And he would start talking to himself.

At twenty-two, soon after he had graduated from one of those colleges where presidents of this country are educated, he made a million dollars in stocks and could have become a rich and powerful man, but he had given it up to marry his second wife, the young writer, Pati Cumberbirch, who later went on to win a National prize. I was surprised to learn this; there were no traces of her in the places he lived, only her book, *Flat Sparrows*, with her picture, a lovely blond woman with red lips fashionable twenty years ago.

They had both gone to live by the sea, she to write — and this surprised me ever more — my friend to write also. Something he always wanted to do, he told me then. In fact, he published stories in two small magazines — the theme was the same; a young man who on a quest is lost and finds himself in a beautiful hidden place where he remains — but he is always forced to return to his former life.

There was something old-fashioned about his writing, as if he still listened to the sound of Tennyson's voice. It was her success, I discovered, that broke up their marriage. How, I really don't know. But he told me, "There's not much lyricism left in a successful writer." As if he were letting me into the privacy of his life, he added, "I should have gone to Paris then. I'm sorry I missed that; being in Paris in my twenties . . ."

One of the most interesting things that happened to me in that time was the arrival of a letter from a city not far from my Mediterranean town. It was from a woman who wrote, *I realized that recently you must have had your sixty-fifth birthday and it must be a difficult time for you, and you must be in need of some comfort. Let me tell you, I could take up with you as if the fifteen years had not passed since you told me that I was too young and that your loyalty would not permit you to love me.*

The letter prompted me to call Jeanne. Bob answered. I had never heard his voice before. His metallic "Hello" nudged me out of the state of well-being the letter had put me in. Bob's voice was so different from Jeanne's. For a moment I said nothing.

"Hello," he repeated. "Hello."

"May I speak to Jeanne?" I finally said.

"Honey, it's for you," his voice fading into what I now felt to be an intimacy of theirs.

I waited. His voice was the voice of a salesman in bad times.

"Hello," Jeanne's voice vibrated in my ear, husky with a slight question at the end of the "Hello?"

She was so different in the presence of Bob. She was subdued, as if resigned to being dominated by a man. It was a shock to hear that in her voice, to see it. Because in that time Jeanne was many things: a free spirit, a fury, a woman of politics, a social butterfly, a lustful wench, a woman capable of writing, a wit, a rascal, flighty, loyal.

With Bob she was the submissive housewife, doing his errands, making his suppers, doing the dishes while he dozed with cans of beer, exhausted from a day of taking on the frustrations of retarded children. I saw her washing his socks and underwear.

Jeanne was settling into her future and I wanted, just then, to convince my friend that he should do everything in his power to see that Bob was convicted. He had, I was sure, sold heroin. How many lives had he ruined? Jeanne would be destroyed in a few years. But I remembered an expression from my Mediterranean town in which I found much truth at that time: "Each head has its own tribunal." And I simply watched.

86

William often said that he was conceived in Paris, on the rue Servandoni. "That's where my troubles come from." I took it lightly at first. It was his way of talking. But after being left all his papers, I think I understand.

His father had been an aviator in the great war, just having the time to arrive at the front in June 1918 and acquiring a reputation as a wild flyer who wept when the war ended. He returned to develop as a hockey player, marry, and wander around Europe with great sums of money he had made with early advice on stocks. He was to lose it all, except for a trust fund for my friend. He was forced to take a job selling champagne, which permitted him to return to

Paris where, on a "heartbreakingly lovely spring day at the age of forty-eight he jumped into the Seine." His body is buried at Chateau Thierry, about three-quarters of an hour from Paris.

My friend was uneasy about approaching forty-eight; not that he feared a temptation to take his life — just approaching forty-eight. I think that's why so many of his letters to Jeanne were addressed, *Dear comfort* . . .

"I should have gone to Paris in my twenties," he often said. "I missed that. I should have gone."

87

In the evening when the wind died down and all was still, the earth was green and splintered and the sky clear blue; then each leaf was in focus, each mountain. There were no shadows. The air was sharp and every leaf and mountain had a sound as limpid as an open memory, the shadows of half forgotten, half remembered love. Then the still air was pulsating with sound that was more seen than heard. One felt like a deaf musician who could not sing, or a painter whose dead eyes had found another way of feeling the things he loved; this earth, these hills, the vein-filled leaves, my gentle friend and Jeanne.

To love people as abstractions with no need to touch them, not to demand emotions from them, is good as you grow old. I loved my friend as friend; Jeanne as life itself and the earth, for what it was.

88

Prudence Ives was the first to call Brian when he returned from India and they both spent nights together after she had made dinner for him of delicate scallops and mussels stewed in rice, and mushrooms (all set between candles) served with a local white wine.

Prudence was a talented pianist who attempted twice to kill herself, once with Doredins and the other by running her small car through an empty store front. This second attempt had left her face scarred and prone to twitching when she became excited. The first attempt had left her furious with those who had saved her life, so that now her humor was hatred disguised as wit. No one escaped her wrath, least of all Brian, whom she loved with a passion, for it seemed to her he was the thing that kept her in this world. It was understandable then, if one night after not hearing from Brian for three days, she came out to the house on Vernon Lake and, at the sight of the diffused red light in his room which she knew he turned on only when he was engaged in love making, she began to call gently as she tapped on the door, "Brian, Brian, it's me."

The silence of that red light hardened her. She began to pound on the door, "Brian. Brian, I know you're up there." Still no answer. She stepped away and shouted up to the window, "Brian, I know you're up there." Her voice vibrated as if she had stepped on a treble cord. " A . . . and you, you bitch, if you think you're going to make it with him . . ." Not finding the words, she bent down and found a stone and then another and began throwing them at the side of the house. With each stone she grunted out a sob until she hit the window, then another, until all three windows were broken. Her face twitching, her eyes wild, her red hair matted to her face, she brought a huge stone up from the boat landing, screaming, "If you think you're going to make it . . . you have a problem. He has a small pecker and doesn't know where to put it."

With a great effort she threw the stone against the large picture window just beyond the screened-in porch. Miraculously the stone bounced off the window and crashed through the porch floor. She fell to the ground crying, and stayed there until William coming home found her and took her home.

To be in love is to risk madness, willingly — The Demon winks.

89

In my Mediterranean town the two sisters I knew were once one lovelier than the other. When young, their bodies were like one strong muscle, their shoulders slightly stooped, as if their breasts were too heavy for them. Graziella, the elder, had chestnut hair, thick as the manes of those horses that run wild in the hills. Melita had black hair and solid white teeth on which she could grind wheat grains into flour.

They were both a joy to be with and their laughter, their singing, filled the house from the time they awoke to the time they went to bed. They never married because they could not find men suitable to their station. The men they loved, after catching a glimpse of them in church, were below their station in life. The men the family desired for them were far above them. They lived out their lives in a fortress of a house with small high windows and stone floors, rearranging the rush bottomed chairs around the wall, for guests that never came. They accommodated though, with such small pleasures as sucking snails their brother brought after a rain and throwing the shells at the outside world.

Melita is dead now. And Graziella is white-haired, her complexion still fine, her eyes red and watery from the many times she threw her stone at the world, as they say in my Mediterranean town.

90

Debrah talked endlessly about others for fear that one would talk of what she believed to be her secret. Because of this, she was a good source of information.

If my friend William suggested — as he did soon after he realized that she had used him — that her love of Brian had turned into a form of revenge, saying, "How else can I explain your determination to sleep with all and any of his friends?" she would interrupt in her rapid lisping voice, "All Brian's friends really want to sleep with Brian and instead they sleep with me," and she moved away as if expecting abuse.

I told her that this was a complicated way of thinking when she began coming to my house to take showers, saying, "The pipes are broken at my place." She would ignore it and lounge around in Brian's multicolored robe. Her love for Brian had shriveled to an obsession. "He'll learn to consider me a woman and not a child as soon as he sees that all his friends consider me a woman," she'd say.

In the meantime her green-almond completion was turning sallow, her smile, too quick; her secret, she thought, was at the edge of her skin and it seemed to her that everyone was at the point of discovering it.

My friend William one day called her a moral slut because she used everyone and herself to feed that weakness, her self-indulgent love for Brian that had turned to hatred. But then my friend was in bad straits.

91

An extraordinary thing happened. One night when my friend William was grieving more than usual and drank too much in the presence of Debrah and Chris, of the small mouth that opened like a flower, and not knowing who had asked and who had consented the three of them ended up in the large bed, furiously thrashing at each other's hurriedly uncovered bodies for two hours, each for their own purposes, each lost in the pleasure of his own anger, until my friend dressed silently, his fingers swollen and numb and left with "the sour-sweet taste of semen in my mouth and not much lyricism, none at all."

Debrah quickly told Brian that my friend had cuckolded him. It was Brian's word *cuckold*. It was extraordinary. Brian who hid himself among women felt cuckolded, because my friend had slept with two women he had known some time ago.

"I feel like a pimp," he kept repeating at dinner. "Your interest in our friendship is that I can attract women for you. I feel like a fucking pimp. A cuckold pimp."

And before we had finished the bottle of wine he muttered, "A shadow has passed over my soul."

It was no use my friend telling him, "I was drunk and depressed. It was a stupid thing to do. I'm sorry. I shouldn't have done it. I'm in love and I shouldn't have done it."

"My ass . . . In the meantime you got a good piece — pieces."

"Brian. They just wanted to get at you. If anyone was cuckolded, I was."

"My ass . . . a man's head is in his cock."

We fell into a long deep silence.

In my Mediterranean town men lower their heads when a friends's wife passes by. It's understood that cuckoldry can happen in a glance — a spasm. The more things change or seem to change the more they remain the same, as they say.

92

In my Mediteranian town the widow's son developed quickly under the guidance of the master painter and within six months was drawing pictures of thorn-covered cactus curved to protect young tomato plants. The thorns were so vivid one could have bled to touch them. He hardly spoke to the painter and took his advice and encouragement with a nod of his head. When the widow came to be the painter's housekeeper the boy grew sullen and sat in the corner whenever the painter told his story — his sullen eyes watching him intently, as if from beneath the shelter of a cactus.

93

I found Alice Mary and Elvira sitting on the small porch with squat, eggshaped tennis rackets in their hands resting gently on the floor. It was a warm night. The crickets made the air whir with sound. From time to time Alice Mary would let go with an old fashioned forehand that ended up way over her head or Elvira would lift her racket and hold it parallel to the ground, her wrist stiff, her eye on some imaginary ball that had passed her years ago.

I came to ask them if they would be character witnesses for Bob — Bobby, really, for they had taught him piano as a child and he had pleased them by playing Rousseau and Scarlatti from his buttocks. He was their baby. How could it be otherwise, when his life was but one-tenth of theirs . . . What is he charged with?" Elvira asked.

"Trafficking in drugs. Hard drugs. Heroin."

"Dear me," she said and swatted at the air as a shadow darted by us. I heard it flutter and for a moment I thought it was a badminton birdie they had been hitting before I came.

"What can we do?" Alice Mary asked.

"You have both been here for a long time. You have done good things for this town. If you said that Bobby was a good boy in what you know about him, it would help."

Alice Mary in a snap of a back hand hit a dark shape. I heard a low ping of her loosely strung racket and at my feet was a bat, its umbrella wings open, its small fangs resting on the wooden porch. Alice Mary stepped on its head and kicked it onto the snow on the mountain that surrounded their house.

"Oh, we'll come, we'll come and be witnesses," Elvira said.

"Yes, of course." Alice Mary nodded and dozed off.

Elvira lifted her racket to shoulder level and with a blocking action let another bat run into the strings. It fell stunned at her feet. She hit it squarely on the head, scooped it up on the racket and flipped it into the darkness.

"Three to two, mine," she said to Alice Mary who woke and said, "Aren't these animals a nuisance, really?"

I left them both and as I walked away they were swatting at the darting shadows, Alice Mary hitting, Elvira pointing to the sky, and then both flaying at the shadows that flitted around their heads.

94

"*Love is truth that can't be put into words,*" my friend wrote.

Jeanne and William believed this. They found it in the confusion of lovemaking and it upset them.

One afternoon he was seized by such a growing fury while making love to Jeanne that he turned her this way and that, stood her up and with breathless gestures turned her right and left, his palm supporting her cunt and each time she whirled around he slapped her body to him with the sound of kneading dough, over and over again. Now his ball bearing plug, a swivel in her, and she, a wet socket to his plug until Jeanne became so frightened and joyful, that she cried with fright, softly, "I trust you. I trust you. Do anything you want to me," until they both clung to each other, wet and trembling. Jeanne began vibrating to a sound my friend's pulsating plug uncovered deep inside her. She began humming — soon moaning.

There was an explosion in the room. Jeanne rolled away, moaning, "Oh, let's get out of here, let's leave this place," and shrank away to the top of the bed, staring at its center as if she saw something terrifying there.

My friend watched her from the floor where he had been thrown. He put his hand on her, "Easy, be quiet."

"Let's leave this place!"

"Easy. Be quiet my heart. Be quiet."

"I've never made love like this before, never."

"Yes, I know," my friend said and went beside her. He waited until her breath came naturally again, to kiss her frightened and angry eyes.

What frightened them both in that wild confusion, I believe, was their conviction that what they had experienced was the truth, and if it were, then they must both be living a lie.

95

"There are some things that frighten me," Jeanne said.

"It had begun too gently. He was in that chair looking at me with that great warmth he can throw at you. 'Come sit here,' I said, and then we were on the floor. I was vibrating; his smell covered me. I was gushing between my legs, something frozen in me was melting, his palm splashed between my legs. Then he lifted me up, my legs were rubber. I fell against him, he turned me, my ass against him. He was huge and throbbing, and I didn't know he was in me. I was so wide and open until he pulled his cock out and I felt so empty — wide and empty — I gasped. He turned me around and then the winding began in me. I was scared. "Do anything you like to me." He was in me, he turned me and he was out. I was gasping for breath. I came on the floor like a cow. But I felt no release. I could stand only because his cock held me up. I was a swivel on it.

"I felt the humming in the back of my knees. It came up my thighs, humming, humming, my stomach tightened. I heard sounds of small explosions and then, bang, something blew up and I was up against the wall looking down at him broken on the floor. He was screaming in pain.

"I knew there was someone else in bed with us, there in the impressions left in the center of the bed.

"I was terrified with the humming in me that would not stop. "Let's leave this place," I kept saying. He was kissing my eyes there. He didn't say a word. He was pulling strings in me and set tops spinning. I felt hollow, wide open . . .

"There are some things I'd rather not know even if they are the truth. Because some things are true. They just are."

Love had come too late in my friend's life. This made him frantic. Bob could have been my friend William's son and Jeanne his daughter. Bob was ready for a helpful friend, not a wife, not Jeanne.

William realized that Bob had married Jeanne because she attracted people to their house; couples, other women, other men. Bob needed people around him, always. Alone with Jeanne, after hastily making love, he fell asleep. Bob had come to settle in this town after what he called a pin-ball machine existence. He had moved from town to town with his father who was a colonel in the army. The moves were sudden jolts, usually after two or three days' notice. Now all he had to show for it was a slight accent in speech from the South and an impatience to get things done with.

He married Jeanne in the city hall of this town, hurriedly, with a few friends and relatives present. In the afternoon he was bar-tending. His education was something to be done with. Now he worked with slow children and he was in a hurry to have them learn and see the day done with. Only when the house was filled with people drinking and shouting did he forget that time for him was a tension to be passed over as quickly as possible. After such parties he would collapse in the bed, to fall asleep innocently while Jeanne remembered the humming rising over her warm and faintly damp body.

It's not that youth is wasted on the young; it's that only the old can see how poignantly beautiful they are. It was not easy for Bob, who wanted everything done with, to have his trial postponed; he wanted it over with. He simply said, "Fuck it." And if Jeanne insisted on making love, he stuffed her cunt with cotton, afraid to tell her that in that time he simply couldn't.

Such things, if they happened in my Mediterranean town, were not talked about.

97

In the evening of the second day of the Feast Day of the Dead, the Master Painter would continue his story. "I became uneasy, really, the way I felt about discovering the strange similarities in the murders, the two bodies, one on the floor, the other on a table, made me believe that it was more than coincidence. I began to look at the newspapers of the past in that great library and found that on the 5th of September ten years to the day, in Paris, there had been a murder of a young woman whose body was found in a *patisserie* on the table and beside her on the floor the body of another, murdered months before — her throat cut.

"I thought it might have been the same assassin, but when I found exactly the same murders committed on September 5th every ten years going back seventy years, I knew that was impossible.

"What could I do? Who could I tell of this? And who would believe me? The idea, that every ten years two young women were found dead on the exact day and in exactly the same circumstances took hold of me as an obsession. Those paintings of bodies trampled beneath the feet of city dwellers came from that obsession. The large haunted eyes I found appearing on all the faces I painted thereafter came from that idea that settled in my head and would not let go of me. Was it my imagination or a quirk of fate? The paintings were sold for very high prices in the cities where those murders had taken place: four in Paris, six in Germany, and five in England. And because those paintings were bought, I painted more, and the more I painted, the more that mystery obsessed me. As the eyes obsessed me. I could not send enough paintings to those cities. To this day they call me for more from Munich. Who would have figured to himself that the conjunction of the stars could have made those events come together once again aboard an ocean liner coming to the Mediterranean from across the Atlantic, where no such murders had ever taken place?"

98

May I tell you both something? I was fifty-five when my wife Susan died. I've never remarried nor have I known or had a desire to know another woman. We had been married fifteen years. It had begun between us as a mindless love and we lived happily, so happily — peeling petals off each other to discover loving comforts in the folds of one another's life. We were aware of it. It's not that now I'm looking back that makes it seem too sweet. We were aware of it, our happiness. Susan died when she was forty, not in an auto accident, or plane accident, or shot; but a natural death. She died of cancer on sheep skin sheets to protect her flesh from her own bones.

I never married again. Why? I just could not go through such a loss again. And what would become of that mindless love of ours if I were to repeat it. I haven't energy, for one. No, I'm not interested in boys. Nor in suffering. I prefer to live this way, with friends, my work — when I was working. You get your turn at things and it's no use being hoggish. There is no end to hoggishness.

I wanted to write about my loss. At the time I felt as if the story was worth telling because it would teach others some profound truth about how we live. But I didn't.

Why?

Because before a blank sheet of paper I discovered it sounded so commonplace and yet so private. I felt disloyal to Susan.

When I walk along the river with Jeanne, who would ever know that I once loved Susan with a mindlessness that was equal to the mindlessness of my friend. Susan loved me with the same assurance. The last thing she said to me was, "Thank you for your company."

Where does love go to in time and space —
nowadays?

99

The mornings began to be cool and suddenly one
day in August the afternoon shadows were longer. In
the evening there were crisp patches of light across
the Lake Vernon, clear light between the branches
where darkness used to be.

Then my friend had to decide whether he would
be a character witness in Bob's favor. It was hard for
him. Because he knew if Bob were convicted, Jeanne
would come with him; if he were acquitted Jeanne
and Bob would go out West. My friend knew his po-
sition in town would decide it. He brooded over it,
telling himself, "I have no right to intrude." Yet if he
did not, he would profit from it. "To do nothing
would be unfair." Both loved Jeanne and "it would
be stupid to let her go with that young fool."

It was then that he began to think in generations
as if they were impenetrable, that he was meant to
come in with people of his age and go out with them,
to intrude, to penetrate into another generation
would be unnatural. He felt this when he heard
Bob's voice or when he walked with Jeanne on the
streets of our town. My friend William's dilemma
would have been unheard of in my Mediterranean
town.

The lady Irish poet had been chosen as a character witness because Judge Elliot considered himself a St. Patrick's Day Irishman. And if in her brogue she were to say that Bob was a good man, how could he reason otherwise?

The lady Irish poet had loved two men in her life: one a married black man whom she had met in Ireland, and the other my friend. She loved my friend William with all the heartfelt panic of loneliness, of one who wrote poems as plaintive cries of help — she showed no one.

Each time she entered her small apartment under the eaves of an old wooden house she felt as if she pulled a trap door down over her head. The ticking of the clock became explosions, the silent telephone made her cry. She'd call my friend at one, even two, in the morning. "Please come and see me. I hate talking into this black thing."

Numb as he was at that time, my friend would dress and go to comfort her, telling her, "I'm in love. I'm in love. I can't divide myself just now."

That was enough for the lady Irish poet. She'd take a pill and go to sleep.

It was understandable then, if our lady Irish poet always had shining moist eyes and a small painful smile on her bony face. She cried for us all at funerals, because she saw the loneliness of death. She cried for herself at weddings because she saw her own loneliness. She was always the first to cry and the first to smile. She seemed to mourn and, on rare occasions, smile for all of us, as poets often do.

101

It was only later, when my friend William's papers were left to me, that I understood his dislike for Debrah. She was friendly with Jeanne and liked her very much. "There's a charmer I've gotten to know, a lovely woman . . ."

William did not want Debrah to know he knew Jeanne. Debrah would be capable of doing her harm. She had a shrew's tongue. Her father moved in the circle of judges, lawyers and politicians who controlled this town on whims. Then, too, the winter Debrah had spent comforting my friend, he was often struck by the realization that he was one year older than her father. Often, when he met him thereafter, he felt indifferent towards this man, then almost a pity as he watched him sitting nervously his reddish wig thick on top of his sallow face.

102

Jeanne and my gentle friend never tired of looking into each others' eyes intently, like two serious children searching one another for solutions to a puzzle.

It was this eye gazing that made my friend William come to a decision about testifying in Bob's case.

They were sitting by the lake, hidden in a cove. Jeanne was holding his arm and he touching her face. They were nose to nose, Jeanne looking into his eyes and my friend, from time to time, backed away as if he feared what she might see there. From a distance it seemed as if Jeanne were pursuing him. She laughed. "Stop it."

"What's wrong?" he asked seriously.

"Your eyes. They're so strange."

Their reasons might have been the cause of his clemency. But I don't think so. You see, on his vacation, Judge Elliot met a young woman with whom he fell in love, the Demon's gift is offered even to judges in their forties. He was too simple a man not to realize that it was his happiness, his exhilarating happiness, which made him, in a cheerfulness he could not control, intone: "Six months in prison which, in light of your favorable witnesses, I suspend . . ."

William had left soon after his testimony had been taken, not looking back, as if he had known the judgment in advance. But, then, he knew this town and how it functioned. He left too, because he felt uncomfortable, to see Bob surrounded by his sister and his brother-in-law, as if he understood there, that if he had seen his relatives every day, this could have never happened.

Bob surrounded by his family quietly walked out of the court room like old couples being remarried, Bob smiling, to the small blue car where Jeanne sat crying.

103

"Did I tell you about my leap for life?" Jeanne told me one evening. "It was last summer when William was away and I was working in Fantasy land. I came home late and I never felt so alone. God, I missed your friend, his talk and his touch. I didn't want to see Bob. I was so confused. I knew there was no future with your friend, but I loved him. I lay in bed naked. The warm summer wind blew over me and that night I just wanted to die. I wanted to kill myself. My life was so absurd. I felt myself dead and I felt a relief. I had accepted it and I was scared. I knew I was going to do it. Anything rather than that vibration all over, my toes twitching, my shoulders aching, the buzzing in my head and my hands shaking. The weed taste of all the cigarettes I had ever smoked. I was scared as I dressed to walk to the throughway and step in front of a car. I put on my pants. I remembered your friend's touch and I lay down with fright and I began to feel my cunt. I grew excited. The wind played with me and I felt myself grow wet. I pressed down on the hard string I felt in me — turning it round and round until I felt the top beginning to spin in me. I felt myself growing a long string to an explosion and then I came and came and stars seemed so tranquil. I had leaped for life so sweet, life is good . . . I'm an old masturbater, you know."

The last time I saw Jeanne she had turned her head and smiled and I could see in the discolored corner of her eye-tooth the black mark of the start of decay.

"She'll write. She'll call. She'll call before she goes," my friend William said.

I sadly bet another bottle of champagne.

"But what makes you so sure each time," he said, "that she won't call?"

"Because of the way she walks, her hair to the wind . . ."

"What do you mean?"

"It's simple. Each time I saw her walk across the bridge over the River Dunbar, and I saw her many times, not once did she look back," I told my friend. "But, then she walked as if she wanted no part of her past . . ."

"And yet I saw that in her wake there was her loving future . . . ," my friend said forlornly.

I said nothing.

104

Jeanne's leaving was an uncoiling of two memories — the detaching left raw wounds.

"I'll put things in boxes and just go," she said. What she put in those boxes was five years of dinners with my friend and Brian, good talk, four years of the jungle war and candlelight marches to the happy beat of young voices singing — a sense of love . . .

Jeanne left us all for the West, Denver or California, wherever love goes to bask in the sun, evaporate and wake up sixty in a small town by the beach.

Jeanne left us on a Sunday morning to the applause of heavy rain. It was full summer and yet I felt as if it were November.

"Don't look like that," she said to me. "Life is full of surprises" and with that good smile added, "and you know that if you live long enough, everything will happen to you." There were tears in her eyes; she wasn't one to cry easily. "I know. I know," I said.

She walked across the bridge that spans the River Dunbar; she walked slowly, lightly. I thought she would turn and wave goodbye. But she walked as she always had, confidently looking ahead, until she turned the corner of a dark red building and disappeared.

105

In the empty theater of my Mediterranean town the painter would go on with his story. "The year 1974 took me across the Atlantic. When I had to return, because I was tired I took a ship one that left in the late summer, August 29th to be exact. The sun was warm and the sea as calm as one of those huge lakes deep in the woods; they call them ponds over there.

"Now, I, on board a ship, I always felt detached from the world. No one from land could reach me and I could reach no one for days. The gentle motion of the ship, *quasi* like the breathing of the earth itself was soothing — as soothing as the routine of eating at appointed hours and siestas in the sun with people who without thought or care in the world, were friendly.

"The first day out I made the acquaintance of a girl called Joan, we would say Giovanna, of a beauty that was extraordinary. Her hair was sometimes red, other times auburn. She was radiant, perhaps twenty-three years old and seemed drunk on life itself. She came from a city by a lake called Dunbar.

"Each morning she came to sit by my side in the sun and tell me of her evening escapades. She had fallen in love with the bartender, a certain Giorgio, while seeing Jiuliano the deck steward in the afternoon. The third day out she became enamored of Giovanni, her waiter, who was, she said, a poet — a mystic. 'He reads to me and is so gentle, not like Giorgio who bit my lip until it bled.' A temporary insanity had taken hold of her. 'But what are you doing to yourself?' I said to her. 'I don't know,' she said. 'It's nice to be in love each night,' and she yawned.

"Through a young man whom every one called J.C., we learned that the ship was carrying a stowaway and the corpse of a young woman. She was the daughter of a well known American maker of films living permanently in one of our large cities now.

"This J.C. went on to tell us: 'Someone broke into the lower hold last night, the coffin carrying the girl from Dunbar Lake was half pried open.' All in fondling a tube of pills he carried in his hands.

"Late that afternoon lying in my cabin I realized that we would be passing the 5th of September on board that ship with the corpse of one girl from a city which Joan came from. I was frightened to the marrow of my bones.

"I jumped to my feet and went to the purser's office. Before the clerk I couldn' t say a word. What was I going to tell him; that for 200 years on September 5th of the fourth year of the decade two girls were found dead?

"To make conversation I asked him, 'In the case of a crime such as the stowaway's, who is responsible for pursuing the criminals.'

" 'Eeh,' he said to me, 'on board ship no one has a desire to violence. The atmosphere is too tranquil — but in the stowaway case — the purser.'

"With the purser at the bar I chatted about violence and after the second drink he said, 'As in the case of the girl who was murdered, her throat cut, and whom we are transporting now . . .' I didn't hear the rest.

"It was 5:30 when I went up to the sundeck where we usually sat. Joan wasn't there. She wasn't in her cabin. I searched all the bars and could not find her. No trace of her. She didn't appear for dinner. At eight I went to her cabin. I knocked endlessly and there was no answer, and then I walked the ship looking for her.

"On the central staircase I met J.C. who had not seen her all evening.

"If you see her, tell her I'm looking for her," and I ran up on the promenade deck. It was deserted, except for an old man who walked hurriedly round and round. The wind was strong and warm on the deserted deck, although as my eyes became accustomed to the dark I thought I saw shadows of couples huddled in the corners. The sea beyond the rails was black in the moonlight.

"At the other end of the deck, I saw the figure of a woman swaying at the railing and leaning into the wind. Bending my head against the wind, I walked towards her. When I got there, she was gone.

"Joan, Joan," I called softly. Nothing. Then I heard the footsteps of a heavy-footed person coming up the gangway. A huge bearded boy passed me, said nothing and disappeared behind me. I looked down the deck below and just then the lights illuminating the fin-backed smoke stacks went on, for the costume ball that evening, and there was Joan looking up at me over her shoulder. She was smiling."

106

This town is filled with once ambitious men who have failed, as they say in my Mediterranean town — men who once were filled with great and vague ambition directed at everything: the lakes, the rivers, the forests, and finally at one another, an ambition so great it stretched them all beyond their limited abilities. The men who built the bridge across the River Dunbar were the last to set their ambitions within the limits of their means, and there is a harmony from the center of the bridge so that now and then I hear a humming there.

My friend William understood this once Jeanne left; his own emotional ambition was greater than his ability and it was an emotional ambition directed at everything: amassing money, painting, writing, and loving women. In Jeanne he believed he had found his limits or someone equal to his enormous emotional ambition, and this made him at once exhilarated and frightened. The good man realizes this and finds his limits early. The prosecutor Sewall, who was not a very bright man, was taken by the possibilities of this town with its abundance. He was angered by Judge Elliot's decision, but this too subsided. They both belonged to the Grand Old Party and Judge Elliot saw to it that the prosecutor Sewall was nominated for the state legislature, the first step of an ambitious man.

Bob's freedom, my friend's bearing witness, Sewall's nomination, all this was done in the name of fraternity. But, then, I've seen men in my Mediterranean town give up freedom in the name of fraternity, as Jeanne gave up her freedom as a woman — freedom, that private place in her radiance that made her ambition equal to her enormous possibilities. She gave that up for the fraternity of a marriage.

107

Abstraction! I understand abstractions. I'm an old masturbater you know, Jeanne wrote to William.

Have our memories become one? The first feeling of becoming me in thinking about you was in my childhood. I found you then within the weave of the wicker chair, painted white and rocking empty in the shade of an old maple tree. It was in the summer of then — *but it goes beyond this town. I know so little of time and history but I am aware of the generations built within me. I am a continuum of memory, of the summer maple darkness. I know it is in the darkness of the tree* — *cavern's walls, where deep symbols of love and life are carved in primal fashion, truth. I'm sure those pallid learned men would have it all summed up in the womb. But, God, it goes way deeper than that, no? My mind runs on. I find you in the same shade spreading on the world. Immediately I find you within the flash of some heat that clapped against the white charcoal metal brim of a Mediterranean man's hat* — *a painter with a hazel-nut face and who smelled of the sea and male mermaids. I knew you then. I discovered you in the mist of countless brewing teas and again on a dark cool welcoming cliff away from the skulls of ani-*

mals at my feet in the marshy boneyard. Soon I saw you between the feathers of a swan and in St. Stephen's green. In Palermo, a petal of red in planted boxes along narrow climbing alleys — and then in the shade of Kronborg castle. Is this shade you? Am I suggesting Death? I've always been in love with the mystery of life. I would like to go to church on some sunny afternoon and be sure to find you there. You are the mosaic in the blossom of my memory. I touch the cordite of my cloistered clitoris, the blossom turns pink. The caverns of my mind explode.

108

The old maple, its pink flesh showing beneath the elephant hide, stood by the River Dunbar, halfhidden, as if ashamed for having out-lived Tom Paine. It was seven feet in diameter and it took me, Jeanne and my friend all holding hands to form a ring around it. It had five branches, each a trunk in it self. Its left, outer-most branch was cemented and broken where once a swing rope had hung, when the Wheeler farm came down to the river.

The old maple was set in the hollow to the right of the bridge. It towered over the black alders and shaded the bridge. It was the oldest living thing in this town, older than the city hall, the monument to a battle, the bridge or the prosecutor Sewall and all the founding fathers. Its presence was noted in at least five deeds.

109

Just after Jeanne left, our conversations at Wednesday dinners, even with Brian there, were quiet as kitchen conversations. William looked grey and swollen. There often was a moist gloss of perspiration on his forehead. We had dinner and quickly left.

One evening William came to me with a small swelling just below his ear, puffy, that made him look like a parrot. He seemed cold and there were yellow hues in his face. He may have been drinking.

The next few days the swelling increased and he grew even more yellow around the eyes. All the doctors told him, "a case of parotitus" the saliva gland, calcified, had become infected — "Common among men of your age" could not convince him that it was not an infection gotten from Jeanne's "sweet parts."

The doctors thought the gland could be drained from the small tit inside the mouth where saliva enters the mouth, the tit through which my friend was convinced the infection had entered his gland. But the gland continued to swell until it looked like a sausage running down from behind his ear.

That last Wednesday, as he ate, I saw his ear redden, then the side of his neck and face turned the color of pomegranates. He began to run a low-grade fever and the next day he was taken into the hospital. "Just to keep an eye on you," a short fat doctor said.

110

We all went to see my friend in the hospital — Brian, Debrah, Nancy and her children and I.

I remember him propped up in bed, looking yellow as old ivory now, saying, "Hi, so, you've all come to see me and you've brought me armagnac. No, they won't mind. Why should they? They have more pleasant drugs. I call out pain and they bring me peace."

Within a week he had lost some weight and he laughed, "No, it's nothing. Just an infected saliva gland."

Then, suddenly, a look of pain came on his face. "They used me, didn't they? Jeanne and Bob. They used me to pump life into their relationship." He was crying. "We old men are so vulnerable, aren't we?"

I didn't have time to answer. He caught himself, cleared his throat, took a deep breath. "Well, no use being hoggish, as you say."

He pinched his nose, took another deep breath, "They're going to operate tomorrow. They tell me... You know they keep saying, 'It's not like your life were in danger.' The doctor told me that. This morning the nurse told me the same thing. 'It's not as if your life is in danger.'

"But just the same, sometime would you go out and walk along the river to the bridge? Don't mind the *Keep Out* signs. Cross it with someone you like — with those kids you drink armagnac with." His eyes filled with tears. "You know, I've come to love them as if Jeanne and I made them in a wild and joyful explosion of love."

"Your life," the painter would say to the Widow, "has been a simple clear gesture. My life has been long and erratic."

"You mean erotic?" the widow asked.

"I mean erratic, erratic."

"Erratic, erotic , what do these words mean?'

"It is too complicated dear, that's what I mean. My life has been a too complicated gesture."

"Eeh, your honor has had many opportunities and has made the circle of the world."

111

In my Mediterranean town where men have died of appendicitis, as a time when the "stomach turns upside down," my friend would have died. The infection would have traveled up the central nerve, up the back of the head. I knew a man who lingered that way for four months until, in his pain and madness, he had burst it open like a sausage in his own fist and bled to death.

William recovered from his illness. And I lost his friendship, really lost it as one loses a valuable heirloom, not remembering where I had last seen it.

We no longer had dinners on Wednesday night. When he returned from his convalescent trip to the shore, we had dinner that Wednesday night: champagne, salmon, lobster and Boston cream pie. But the next Wednesday, Brian had to be away. Then my friend went to Philadelphia for a week. I had a quiet dinner with Brian. We hardly said a word to each other. As we left, he said to me quietly, "Fucking gets in the way of friendship, doesn't it?" When William came back, we missed an evening. There was a snow storm. Until one winter evening I found myself alone, and neither Brian nor William called. Thereafter when either one saw me walking, he would wave as he drove by. Their greetings became less and less animated, until they ignored me. Then, too, they both bought new cars — William a small Chrysler and Brian a Jeep to help work the land of the commune he was contemplating joining, and I couldn't recognize either one of their cars.

One summer evening Brian, seeing me walking towards him, crossed the street and walked, looking straight ahead of him until he turned the corner.

It was understandable. It was Jeanne who had held us together. And William must have been embarrassed for having made farewell speeches to life too soon.

Brian that year began to lose his hair, no small thing to a man whose only barrier between him and suicide was the continuous exhilaration of beginning love. Brian for a moment was terrified and angry when he saw the large bald spot at the back of his head that appeared, it seemed to him, overnight. His body had betrayed him, failed him, and if it had failed him in producing hair the time was not far when it just might fail him in his kidney or his heart. The last time I caught his eye I knew he would avoid me thereafter. My bald head with its wisps of hair arched up to trace where once my hair stood layer upon thick layer, my sagging face, my white beard, my talk of my Mediterranean town, all this smelled if not of death, then of old age and Brian, I think, was looking forward more to death than old age.

I had not heard from either of them for over a year when I read of my friend William's death and the stipulation of his will in a letter sent to me by a Philadelphia lawyer.

112

It was William's wish to leave me all his personal papers and a sum that would have kept a modest person in good spirits for a year. He left me this sum for the effort of deciding what to do with these bits and pieces of his life, and added that under no circumstances should they be seen by his writer-former wife, Pati.

His estate was divided among a brother in Pennsylvania, his first wife, a woman in Spokane, Washington, three women in this town I did not know, and Nancy.

Why he left me all these documents of his private life, I did not understand at first. There was an unfinished novel, diaries begun on trips he had taken and abandoned after a few pages, a notebook with investment advice he gave himself, observations on people he had known, and many letters from women.

After reading all he had left me, I understood why he had left them to me. No doubt he thought I would be the least embarrassed by this aspect of his life which he wanted not to be forgotten because he considered it to be reality — the rest was illusion. It was part of him he didn't quite understand. He thought I might.

The letters from at least a dozen women covered a period of five years before he met Jeanne. After Jeanne came into his life, there were no such letters, only drafts of letters to Jeanne, in a handwriting that varied from a wide wild scribble angling off in all directions, to the tight writing of an angry bookkeeper.

In that tight bookkeeper hand he wrote:

One thing I've learned from all this, if I'm honest with myself. I've always wanted to be in love, and the older I grew, the more I searched for it. In Jeanne I realized that when it came too late, it was impossible. I walked the streets with her and I felt embarrassed. I realized that I would have been uncomfortable with her — she would be uncomfort-

able with me. It would have blown her friends'
minds she told me, and you, my friend, would have
thought me an old fool. I cried for all that because
to live with Jeanne was impossible; our love could
not stand the light of public . . . Can any love permit
its conversations to be overheard — and then take
them seriously?

In my Mediterranean town this could have
never happened.

113

On the last day of the Feast of the Dead, when the
children of my Mediterranean town find sugar dolls
with smiling red lips on their beds, in the evening
the Master-Painter would finish his story.

"I looked down to Joan in the light. I called to
her, 'Joan, stay there please. I must talk to you. Stay.'

"I ran to the stairwell and as I hurried down I
had the sentiment she would disappear or that she
had not been there in the first place. At the bottom
of the stairs I saw her holding on to the rail — swaying towards and away from the edge as if she were
picking up the movement of the ship.

"She was wearing a full calico skirt, her hair was
blowing over her face.

"Where have you been? I've been looking all
over for you." I touched her arm and for a moment I

had the feeling she would disappear. She was warm as bread from the oven.

" 'Oh I spent the day drinking champagne at a grand buffet of love, in a small cabin and then in a little tepee part of the ship. How do you like my costumes I'm going to the ball as a pioneer woman.' She swayed and almost fell backwards. I caught her. Her champagne breath made her smell of sour dough.

"Joan, *cara* Joan, you might be in trouble."

" 'Oh, come now. I don't like men worriers.'

"But there is good reason to worry. Something is going to happen."

" 'Take care of yourself,' " she said and looked away.

"From the corner of my eye I could see couples in costumes walking in the sheltered parts of the deck.

" 'No . . . You . . . Please stay with me tonight."

" 'I can't.' "

"Just until midnight then."

" 'I have an appointment.'

"At the other end of the deck a slim figure appeared. He was in the shadows and I could not see him clearly. He raised his hand and Joan said, "Oh, there he is now. What's his name?" and started drunkedly to walk away.

"She was already halfway to him when I called out, 'Take care.' I knew she didn't hear me. It was already five past eleven. I watched them walk away arm in arm down to a lower deck where the crew spent their leisure hours sunning themselves on the

cargo hatches. There they sat watching the moonlight on the black sea.

"I crouched half-hidden behind the stacked
deckchairs. I heard footsteps behind me. I turned.
Nothing. When I looked below, I saw Joan stiffen as
the figure pulled her down to the hatch. Sharp points
of light reflected from his face and hands. I heard
Joan cry out, her voice came up to me garbled by the
wind. Then his hand was on her mouth. She must
have bit him for he let go and I heard her scream
again.

"My throat was suddenly dry. I had difficulty
breathing as if my throat had collapsed and its sides
had stuck together.

"For a moment I could not move. Then with an
effort I started shouting like a maniac. I picked up a
deck chair and half threw it, half dropped it at him.
Without looking I went shouting down the gangway
leading to the deck below. I saw the chair hit close to
his feet. His hands were brilliant with bits of light
now. Joan screamed in pain. And as I stood on the
deck, the figure turned to me. His face was masked
with spangled lace tight against his face, like the
scales of a fish. His eyes were long and parrot green,
his small mouth painted red as blood. The wind
lifted the scales of his face and for a moment he
seemed to be twitching. We were all three frozen in
the moonlight. The spangled-faced figure then
looked at Joan beneath him, to me and behind me,
with short sharp motions, that seemed to have no

middle, just beginnings and ends, and in a graceful leap jumped silently over the side.

"I found Joan whimpering on the deck. Her hands cold, her eyes were wide and out of focus, as if pleading to someone I could not see.

" 'You're all right, Joan, all right,' I repeated. She put her hand to her throat and took it away covered with blood. Her mournful eyes looked behind me. I turned and saw the purser and two other men coming toward us."

114

When we got Joan to the ship's doctor he found nothing really serious, only abrasions, as if made by a cheese grater, over her throat and chest.

The next day Joan told me it wasn't anyone she had known before. "He was too made up. I think he said he was going to the ball as a male mermaid. His body was hard and cold and yet warm. The fish scale gloves were like rasps on my throat." She shivered.

Strange though. She had recuperated so quickly from her fear. But then she was strong, appeared to have great strength, or like most people from her part of the world, she quickly forgot the past.

They never discovered who the man had been. Everyone on board ship until we docked was apprehensive. I, for my part, was relieved, although left with a strange sense of harmony. Because soon after, I found the man of science's words, *All that we see*

*and observe has nothing to do with the movements
of planets inspace, but with temporal changes
caused by the stars and this earth in the flow of
time.* I felt something shiver in me.

That Spring the Gruzov Comet, which had been
appearing in the skies for 250 years, changed course.
It caused great consternation among the savants.
There were those who felt that a great catastrophe
would occur; there were others that predicted a new
prophet would appear.

I'm simply awaiting the fourth year of the next
decade to see if this cycle of decade murders has
been broken.

I would like to live that long, but I doubt it, because I feel as if I've offended powers that are more
ancient than any of our God's memory.

115

Among William's papers there was a letter headed
To Jeanne. I don't know if he ever sent it. Much of
what it said made me feel that I hardly knew them.

*You are born with some things and into others;
your temperament, your father's gestures, your
mother's nuances. Accept these things because you
can't do anything about them. Above all, don't fight
them. They love a fight and feed on it.*

*Love and life are the same; if they lasted for-
ever, they would not be as sweet.*

If you have the choice between doing something stupid or doing nothing, do nothing. Most stupidities are done out of boredom or loneliness.

Learn to live quietly with yourself. Then living with others will be a dividend.

Don't pay too big a price for fraternity; often men have lost their freedom in exchange for fraternity.

If mindless love should overwhelm you, consummate it, that is, live in close proximity until it is burned out. Otherwise its possibilities will haunt you the rest of your life and you will move from one phantom to another.

Explanations are to be found in the future as answers are found in solutions — the reason for our love was to be found in our life together. Anxieties are in the future, not in the past. It must be so, because we know we learn nothing from the past in things that really matter. If it were not so, we'd be much happier. You and me.

116

How temporary and fragile this town seems now that my friend is dead and Jeanne is gone. Through both of them I've been given a hint, I feel. It would not take much to have it all disappear beneath a growth of alders, poplars, birch and maple trees.

I often walk along the river, expecting a pang of memory at the sight of the bridge, the ten poplars, the maple and the shore beyond where Jeanne used to walk, her auburn gold hair loose, the sun around her face. But as often as I walk there, I've never felt a thing. The bridge is just a bridge — the trees only trees. It's relationships that give character to men and things — and now I must force myself to think of Jeanne or of my gentle friend William here by the river, as if the place refuses to be filled with their character.

Yet from time to time, in winter, I feel their presence in my room, as if Jeanne were touching my shoulder to say: "Come on, we'll walk by the River Dunbar and across the bridge . . ."

Even these remembrances are becoming less and less vivid and sometimes I have difficulty remembering Jeanne's face or William's gestures. But then, as they say in my Mediterranean town, time is a gentleman and forgives us everything.

117

With the end of the story, an old man, after a long silence asks, "Eeh, Master Painter, did you ever see the girl Joan again?"

"No, I received three postal cards, one from a city not far from here telling me she was experiencing a fabulous story of love, then another saying she was coming to look for me, and the last from Ireland, that she was returning to her home by the river Dunbar in the autumn."

"Eeh, tell us though, did you put it to the girl Joan?"

This was the signal for the master painter to finish a tumbler of whiskey and begin a wild dance to all the dark corners of the theater, a dance that would have been an honor to the great God Pan himself.

END

The Guernica Prose Series

Claude Péloquin. *A Dive into My Essence.* 1990

Pierre Yves Pépin. *American Stories.* 1996

Penny Petrone. *Breaking the Mould.* 1995

Giose Rimanelli. *Accademia.* 1997

Giose Rimanelli. *Benedetta in Guysterland.* 1993 (American Book Award 1994)

Francis Simard. *Talking It Out: The October Crisis from the Inside.* 1987

Stendhal. *The Life of Mozart.* 1991

France Théoret. *The Tangible Word.* 1991

Anthony Valerio. *Conversation with Johnny.* 1997.

Anthony Valerio. *The Mediterranean Runs Through Brooklyn.* 1997.

Anthony Valerio. *Valentino and the Great Italians.* 1994

Yolande Villemaire. *Amazon Angel.* 1993

Robert Viscusi. *Astoria.* 1994 (American Book Award 1996)